Hidden Dragons

Kathleen Osborne

WRITINGS BY K OSBORNE LLC

Copyright © 2024 by Kathleen Osborne

All rights reserved. By payment of the required fees, you have been granted the non-exclusive, non-transferable right to access and read the text of this e-book on-screen. No part of this text may be reproduced, transmitted, down-loaded, decompiled, reverse engineered, or stored in or introduced into any information storage and retrieval system, in any form or by any means, whether electronic or mechanical, now known or hereinafter invented, without the express written permission of the author, Kathleen Osborne.

This is a work of fiction. Names, characters, places and incidents are either the product of the author's imagination or are used fictitiously, and any resemblance to actual persons, living or dead, business establishments, events or locales is entirely coincidental.

No portion of this book may be reproduced in any form without written permission from the publisher or author, except as permitted by U.S. copyright law.

WARNING: Sexual content and violence:

This novel contains some scenes that would be rated R in heat-intensity sexual content.

Note: The intimate scenes may be skipped, but are meant to show a side of the character not seen elsewhere.

Sexual violence is discussed as an exploitation of women and men in the past tense, some as described as flashbacks. These are written to explain the past, and those how would bring the past to the present.

Dedication

My sweet husband of 48 years, Robert. Our children, and their families.
My dear friends and fellow writers of Show Low Writers Group, The Scriptorium Critique Group... without your counsel and encouragement, this book would have never made it to print.

Acknowledgements

I must acknowledge all those individually who helped me get Hidden Dragons published.

My husband, Robert, who listened to me and gave me excellent advice.

My friend, Jonathan Pembroke, who edited it and asked me if I wanted a 'hard look edit'.... and of course I said, 'yes'. His sage advice and recommendations were invaluable.

To my fab beta readers: Stephany Borders, Cassandra Harris, and Mira Young... Their insight was incredibly helpful.

To my proofer, Mir Yash Seyedbagheri, with your help I made it over the last hurdle to help finish Hidden Dragons.

The digital help I used to write and publish came from: CampfireWriting.com, Word.com, ProWritingAid.com, AutoCrit.com and Atticus.io.

One of the hardest parts of writing and producing a novel is the cover. I worked with 100Covers.com; they did a marvelous job.

Every single one of you is incredible. I couldn't have done it without your encouragement.

Thank you!

Kathleen Osborne

Contents

Prologue	1
Chapter 1	18
Chapter 2	24
Chapter 3	35
Chapter 4	45
Chapter 5	54
Chapter 6	63
Chapter 7	73
Chapter 8	88
Chapter 9	100
Chapter 10	113
Chapter 11	123
Chapter 12	137

Chapter 13	150
Chapter 14	157
Chapter 15	172
Chapter 16	183
Chapter 17	198
Chapter 18	211
Chapter 19	223
Chapter 20	237
Chapter 21	248
Chapter 22	255
Chapter 23	258
Chapter 24	269
Chapter 25	279
Chapter 26	297
A Sneak Peek	302
About the author	307

Prologue

Liberty Hospital

Tremors ran through Iona Shelby's body as she snatched up a knife and placed it in a sheath hanging from the back of her belt. She glanced down at her naked hands and muttered, "Can't leave without my punch rings."

Now she is prepared to face the gang she'd have to walk by to get on her bus. *If I ran. They will never catch her.* The temptation was so strong. Her parents' voices were firm. "If anyone discovers what you can do, they'll report you to the authorities. They will hand you over to the scientists. You'll never see us again."

Her older sister said in with her two cents' worth. "Yeah, you've got to keep it a secret. That means you can't use it where any people are around... ever. The big wigs won't care how old you are. They'll make sure you disappear into their labs."

God! Dina is the best sister. She took me in, raised me. Please don't let her die. She was the one who told her the only person stopping her from reaching her dream was herself. For every harsh word said to her from teacher or fellow students, Dina firmly stated, they were wrong, she was capable, enough for any situation. No one had the right to tell her any differently.

Tears welled up in her eyes. She paused on her way out. "Damn it, not now." Blinking them back, she took a deep breath, then released it in slow increments.

She strode to the stairwell and slipped on a half piece of pizza lying in the hallway. What a mess. Scattered bits of trash found in the bathroom and kitchen were everywhere. It was gross. She toed a half-eaten apple out of her way, dashed down the two flights of stairs, dodging used rubbers, dirty nappies.

Something bad must have happened last night.

The community areas were normally clean, overnight someone created a mess.

Hmm. Another gang was probably making a play for the building. It was the only time they ever found trash in the hallways or landings.

The bus pulled up to the curb as her hand hit the front door. She didn't break her stride all the way to her ride. Iona ignored everything else. What mattered was to get on it before it left. It was the only mode of transport available to her.

She boarded the bus, paid her fare, and scanned for a seat. Her eyes locked with the gang leader's intense stare, sending a chill down her spine. His intimidating presence dominated the space. Six-foot-four inches of solid muscle towered before her, his clean-shaven face proudly displaying an array of tattoos. Three tear-shaped marks near his eyes, rumored to represent his kills, stood out starkly. Numbers etched across his forehead hinted at time served behind bars.

The gang leader never strutted or boasted. He didn't need to. His whispered commands sent his men scrambling to obey. Now, his gaze fixed on her, possessive and hungry. Terror gripped her as she realized: in his eyes, she already belonged to him.

Today, for the first time, he wasn't leering at her. He turned a blind eye when his men harassed her whenever she came outside. They were all standing behind him, their gaze centered on him. Her eyes met his. He raised his hand to his forehead, as to salute her. Afraid to do anything more overt, she nodded. Then he did the weirdest thing; he led his followers away.

Why? Did this mean he would leave me alone for the time being. It was weird. Did he know Dina was in the hospital?

The weapons she wore might have made her appear to be ready to take on all comers, but all they did was help hide her emotional state. The fear of not having her sister in her life kept claiming her thoughts. Had the leader known she was all bravado?

A soft touch on her elbow from the driver made her jump. "Thank you." Then she took an unoccupied seat.

There was no noise, just silence as they went to the next stop. The solar-run vehicle was quiet, yet it wasn't obvious until the other passengers started chatting, filling it full of friendly banter.

Relief filled Iona when no one tried to talk to her. It had been a long time since moved from their old neighborhood. Things changed a lot when her sister got her job as an executive secretary. Now they had food and amenities they hadn't had before.

She grimaced at what was available. Little or no meat depending on what you will eat. Butchers prepped everything from rats to dogs and to cats, to the normal farm animals—chicken, pigs, and beef. The scarcity of fresh meat puts the price so high a family of four might get one meal a month with it as the main course.

Vegetables and grains were the main source of sustenance. The moon and meteor dust had done something to the soil, so that they didn't taste anything like when she was kid... at least what was available in the city.

The biggest improvement had been a bathroom in their own apartment. Before they had a communal one for the entire floor. If either of them had to use it, day or night, the other stood guard with a can of pepper spray.

The difference now was huge. Everywhere her gaze traveled, she found construction going on. Buildings that were just shells from the meteor and the moon's debris were being demolished. And new ones were going up.

One high-rise cement with steel girding, and glass building was miraculously still standing from before the catastrophe. She guessed it was fifteen stories high. Sitting with the side of her face against her window and tilting her head up, she saw bits of greenery trailing down from the roof. Maybe from a rooftop garden?

People had their laundry hanging on the rails of their balconies. Her view let her see there were cracks visible from where she sat underneath the cement and steel balconies. A shiver went through her at the thought of something heavy being placed on one of them causing it to rip apart, landing on the unsuspecting people below.

She used the window as a mirror and grimaced. Yeah, the meteor. She'd been very young when it struck the moon, causing a cascading effect on earth. First it pulled the planet off its axis by three degrees, then the volcanoes went off everywhere, nations disappeared, shorelines changed.

When the announcement warned everyone about the coming disaster over the radio and TV, her parents packed their car. And driven her and Dina up to their mountain cabin.

To catch the bus might she have to walk straight out of the building, then she'd have to stroll through the gang that felt the entire place block was theirs.

Her eyes darted from one place to another as people were walking in small groups everywhere. She saw two black cars and two vans painted red and white during the thirty-minute ride. When she was small, those that color had lights on top and sirens. Her mom called them ambulances… vehicles that took hurt people to the Emergency Room at hospitals and had the right of way.

These weren't red, and they had three rows of seats filled with people. The passengers she knew were workforce people. Transportation provided to and from their jobs.

Despite all the improvements she saw, there were still immense problems to overcome. The basic needs—food and shelter weren't being met. Yet, in the last three years, the Internet worked... similar to what it had been.

Now, you had to have a clearance, like a driver's license, to get online. They were expensive to buy. Fortunately, her job paid for hers. Everyone listened to broadcast information, government websites, weather, and to contact police or ambulance. But for anything else you had to be allowed. Even then, you would be limited to using it only during certain hours. With her job, she used it any time because the data she had to do reports on came in throughout the day and night.

When the bus pulled up, the driver shouted, "Liberty Hospital! Anyone going to Liberty Hospital. This is your stop."

Iona flew out of her seat and joined a group of men and women walking toward a doorway with a sign over it: ER Entrance. She stayed at the back. The last thing she wanted was to be caught alone. Her mother told her stories of when it was safe to walk by yourself. By the time she was twelve, it wasn't even safe to be alone with law enforcement officers, unless a woman was one of them.

She let her eye catalog everything she was seeing and couldn't help noticing a parked dark blue sedan across the street from the ER. It was non-descript, very plain vehicle... someone sitting a in car was highly unusual. You had to be rich to have one. The fuel for them was scarce.

Out of the corner of her eye she noticed, when someone came toward the entrance to the Hospital, he'd raise binoculars to eyes. It didn't help that what she saw of his facial expression, cold. He might of have been made of stone. Not someone she wouldn't want to meet by herself.

She stepped into the group and dipped her head, so her hair covered her face as she hunched her shoulders.

Her back was to him as she walked into the ER. She made it all the way to a set of big double doors and a guard pulled her out of the crowd. He told her, "You're not staff, you can't go in there. You need to go to the plexiglass-enclosed counter over there." He pointed at a section on the opposite wall. "And tell them why you are here."

There was a sign on the front of glass with big red letters, "ADMITTING." To the left of a man with long white hair was a stack of clipboards on his other side.

Iona stepped over to the window. "I received a call that my sister has been admitted here. Her name is Dina Shelby. She's pregnant."

The man blinked at her, then picked up a phone from below the counter. "The hit-and-run's sibling is here."

Shocked, she glared at him, and he grimaced back. "Sorry, I thought they would have told you that information. Um, someone is coming to take you to her. Go sit across in a chair where you can see me. I'll tell them where you are."

She blinked her eyes to keep the tears back. No way was that man's callousness going to get to her. She needed to be there for Dina just as she had always been there for her.

A tall, red-haired nurse burst through the double doors and headed straight to admitting. The man she talked to pointed to her, then waved at another person to come to him.

"Miss Shelby, Iona Shelby?" The red-headed man held out his hand toward Iona. "I'm the RN handling your sister's case. You can call me Sonny. The baby is doing well considering. But Miss Dina is in labor."

"Can I see her? I was going to be her birthing coach."

"We'll have to clear that with the doctor."

Sonny led her to a room with a police officer standing outside it, and the window curtains closed.

What the... Police? Here, this is not good.

That man at admitting said it was a hit and run. Do they think it had been deliberate?

She slammed to a halt a few feet from the officer, glared at Sonny. "Why is there a police officer here?"

"This is standard protocol when there is a hit-and-run. The two police came with officers accompanied the ambulance. That's when we were told, your sister was walking down the sidewalk. She had left a store next to an alley. A car came out of nowhere, according to the witnesses, and drove straight at her. She came to us unconscious."

"Are you saying it was deliberate?"

Was this why the man was watching everyone who came in through the ER?

"They don't know, it's just a precaution." Sonny took a step toward the door, Iona put her hand on his arm.

"How bad is it? Is she even conscious?" *What if she can't even talk to me? God, let her be able to talk.*

"The doctor will let you know her condition, and yes, she is awake. She was the one who told us how to contact you. They never found her personal effects at the scene."

"And the baby?"

"As soon as an OR is available, she is going to have a C-Section." He glanced down the hallway. "I see her doctor coming. Let's go in now, so he can answer all your questions."

Stepping into the room, she took everything in a glance. Her sister, Dina, sat up in a bed, her huge tummy sitting on the top of her legs. She had all kinds of medical equipment attached to her. Multiple bandages covering extensive areas of her arms and legs were being monitored by some machine. She had a black eye, with cuts on her brow and lips.

Tears forming in her eyes, she ran to her side and hugged her. Only to receive a tight squeeze from her sister. Dina's gaze went to Sonny. "The doctor just told me he must do a C-section. Before that happens, I need to talk to you and the surgeon." She grabbed Sonny's arm. "My sister must be part of the conversation."

Her eyes widen and her jaw dropped. *Why would she have to be there? Just how serious is this... She can't die. We only have each other.*

Sonny ran off to find him as the two sisters turned to one another. "Please don't talk, just listen to me. Don't interrupt. There isn't much time. Let me say what I need to say, then you can speak, okay?"

Iona nodded.

"I know, because I looked at my chart. They left me alone for a few minutes. One of the nurses left her access card next to the computer. It was close enough for me to get to the keyboard. I hacked into my records. The prognosis is not good. If I don't make it through this surgery, and the baby does, promise me you'll raise her. Say it. I must know you'll do it.

She reached for her sister's hand and nodded. *This isn't happening. You can't leave us... your baby needs you. I know nothing about kids. I can't do this.* She cleared her throat, her voice clogged with unshed tears. "I promise she'll be mine."

"What I'm asking next is very important to me. If I have a son, his name must be Manier, after his father. If I have a daughter, her first name must be Hester, after Manier's mother. Please, will you do this?"

"Yes. I will."

The doctor, with Sonny trailing behind him, came in. He spoke rapidly. "We have to get you into surgery now, Miss Shelby."

"No, not yet." Dina was gripping Iona's hand so tight, she thought it would be black and blue when she let go. "First you have to bring me a paper, and you have to sign as witnesses that my sister will be the guardian of my child, should something happen to me."

The doctor glanced at the nurse. "Take care of it, damn it all."

Iona eyed the clock.

The surgery nurse came in and double-checked Dina's IDs and information, followed by the anesthesiologist. The latter explained who he was and what he would give her, and how it wouldn't adversely affect the baby.

Four minutes later, the last of the OR team put a warm blanket on her sister and left. Then he was back with a clipboard, holding a form with typing on it and a pen in his hand.

He handed it to the doctor, then to her. She saw he typed out her request and dated it. And made a signature block for each one present. Dina signed her name and handed it back to him.

As they took to surgery, the nurse handed Iona the signed document and escorted her to the surgery waiting room.

The clock had to be slow. It seemed like she'd been there a day, not an hour? Her hands were on the chair's arms to stand when Dina's doctor walked in. His serious expression had her out of her seat and walking toward him. She moved so fast she was light-headed.

Instead of speaking right away, he gripped her elbow and steered her to a corner of the room, away from the other people in the room. "I'm so sorry. We did everything possible. But your sister's heart quit. We tried several times to revive her, but nothing worked." He paused. "Your niece is fine. Do you have a name for her, so we can fill out her birth certificate?"

The question grated on her like fingernails on a chalkboard, making her want to withdraw completely from the entire world. She guessed he'd lost no one before... He obviously had no sensitivity training to go with his degree.

She focused on him, attempting to seal off the pain. "Her name will be Hester. Now, when can I see Dina... and the baby?"

"You can go up to the fourth floor any time to see the little one, and tomorrow you can take her home. As for your sister," he paused. "That might be a few days. I'll have the police officer in charge contact you. They will escort you to the viewing area at the morgue."

He inched toward the door. "Any further questions should be directed to the police." He made it clear he didn't want any involvement. He'd done his job, and that's all that needed to be done.

Iona watched the surgeon walk off and turned to face the room. She let them know she was aware they eavesdropped on her conversation with the doctor. The telltale red going up their necks and coloring their faces shouted it to her. All the pain and anguish bottled up inside her, with no place to let it out. She froze for a moment. Casting her eyes wildly in both directions, she looked for help?

I am my own guide... everything for little Hester. She closed her eyes, tilted her face upward. *God, I need your wisdom if I'm going to do it.*

The sound of a door slamming shut startled her from her thoughts.

I need to find out how to get to the fourth floor where they took Hester.

Hester

I ona paused at the stairwell's top, quickly orienting herself. A man caught her eye, flanked by two small boys in dirt-smudged jeans with bulging pockets. One child clung to his left leg, the other wrapped both arms around the other one. The man tapped on a window, facing into the building. He stooped, scooping up both kids, one in each arm. He nodded and smiled at something—or someone—inside. One boy piped up, "Daddy, is that our sister?" The other immediately chimed in, his voice thick with disgust, "Did we look like that, Daddy?"

Okay, that's where they took Hessie. She walked across the tile floor and stood next to the father holding his sons. She had spotted Hessie when one of the nurses waved at her, then gestured she was coming out to the hallway to speak to her.

"Hello, I'm the charge nurse for the nursery. May I help you?"

"Yes, when can I see my niece?... I'd like to hold her." She glanced down, then met the woman's eyes. Warmth and peace flooded her. It was so powerful she had to look away as she cleared her throat.

"Sorry, I'm Iona Shelby, Hester Shelby's guardian. We need some time alone, please."

"Follow me. We have a special room for situations like yours. You can even stay until she is released so we can teach you how to care for her, if you want."

"Thank you, I'd like that."

Ensconced in a small room with a single bed, a crib, and a rocking chair, she held the tiny baby. The nurse had left her with a bottle to give to her when she woke. She gazed down at her niece. "Hester is your name, but I'm going to call you Hessie. And you're going to have to bear with me... I've never even babysat, so I feel so inadequate to care for you. I am so glad you have your mother's blue eyes; I hope they stay that way. Your dark hair must come from your grandma's side or your dad's. Only my mom and I had dark hair. None of that really matters because you are mine, and together we are family."

Hessie stirred, as if she had understood every word she had said. Then cried out, waving her little hands, and kicking with her feet. The nurse had said this would be the signal to feed her. When she latched onto the bottle, she snuggled close to Iona's chest.

As the baby nursed, she released the tears she'd been holding back, and whispered to her niece, "Why would someone want to hurt your sweet and kind mommy?"

Chapter 1

New Rocky Mount, Joint Carolinas, New USA

"Meet the man or the woman of your dreams. Go to '*site.dreammakers.nwdd*,' fill out the form, and we will find *your* perfect match. We'll locate your soulmate. Now, go to, *site.dreammakers.nwdd*."

The television volume reverberated throughout the room as the announcer's voice rose just to soften into a whisper a few seconds later. That and the sound of waves washing up on a shore caught her attention, startling her enough to look at the ad. The soundtrack of the video ensnared her so much she barely registered the couple strolling on a beach. The announcer's voice reverberated through her body, "*Be united with your soulmate now, go to,*" the masculine tones raising goosebumps on her skin.

How strange... was that aimed at her.... No, it wouldn't be, would it?

She picked up the baby food jar and the spoon by twisting at the waist, setting them on the dining room table. *Such nonsense,* she thought, taking the chair next to her six-month-old niece, in her highchair. She lifted a spoonful, touching Hessie's mouth with it. The baby shook her head and threw herself backward.

Crap, the game. Pursing her lips, she started making engine noises and turning the spoon into an imaginary plane, doing swoops and swirls. She lowered her voice an octave and announced, "Coming in for a landing. Open the hangar doors, please." And just like a baby bird, Hessie's mouth opened, letting it land. Once she finished eating, she gave her the spoon to play with. Chuckling, she watched as the baby attempted to put it in her mouth. Instead, she had hit every place on her face before she found her target.

With no warning, a heavy sadness blanketed her. Dina wasn't here to see her daughter see her feed herself. She would have laughed like a loon.

—*Waaaa!*

The cry jerked her out of her musings, and she smothered a smile at the little one's appearance. She sat in her highchair, grinning and naked. Somehow, she had taken all her clothes off by herself. She looked at the image before her.

"Okay, you little monkey, it's almost bedtime. You're getting a sponge bath tonight." Times like this made her grateful for her minuscule apartment. Picking the little one out of her chair, she turned around to get the water running in the sink. Having a tiny apartment had its perks.

After cleaning her up, a glance at the clock told her it was her bedtime. Pulling a bottle from the frig, she warmed it. She rocked Hessie as she let her hold it, as she sang the song her mother had sung to her. "*Nap time, nap time, sleepy little one. Nap time, nap time, rest 'till done. Nap time, nap time, wake to have fun.*"

When she finished drinking, the little one's eyelids closed, and her hands dropped to her side. Iona shifted to her shoulder and burped her. The loud noise made her smile as she rose from her rocking chair, took two steps over to the crib, and laid her down.

While gently covering her niece, she surveyed her abode. Her mother would have told her it wasn't big enough to swing a cat!

She wished they had been able to keep the apartment she and Dina had lived in, but her job paid so much less than her sister's. There was no way she would keep it. She knew she was lucky to find this place. Its locale wasn't the greatest, it was an industrial neighborhood, factories, shipping companies surrounded her building. The bottom floor was a parking garage, and the four floors above it where old offices were converted to studio apartments.

It had all the basic needs, and she had thought it was gang free when she signed her lease. Two days later, she realized it came with a gang that felt anything or one on the block was theirs to hassle. Every time she had to leave her home, they harassed her, to the point she was armed all the time. Each time she had to defend herself brought back some terrifying memories.

It had been two years ago, just two months after moving into their last apartment together, she had a horrifying encounter with a man. Screaming *"FIRE!"* was the only thing that had saved them.

Iona shivered. They'd never caught him. From then on, Dina had insisted she take self-defense classes. And Dina had been so proud of her when she earned her first black belt.

Tears filled Iona's eyes as she thought about it. She still mourned her sister. They had become so close when she became her guardian.

The strains of music announced the ad for .

One step and she was in front of her dresser. She pulled her PJs out and changed clothing. Dragging the pants up to her waist, she let go of them, and they slipped off her hips to the floor. *I've got to get something more to eat. What will happen to Hessie if I die of starvation?*

Minutes after the music had died away from the ad, it repeated a second time.

Weird. Can't seem to get away from it.

Iona's eyes darted between the sleeping baby and the advertisement. *It might be a trap by human traffickers. But would they advertise on TV? It seemed legitimate. The idea of a repulsive partner or a stranger's touch was revolting.* The announcer's voice interrupted her thoughts: "Luxury awaits you; all needs met." She looked around her sparse surroundings, clothes hanging on pegs, mismatched furniture. *No more going hungry to feed Hessie.* The chance for them to eat and stay together silenced her internal debate.

Before she changed her mind, she grabbed her laptop, lifted its lid, and turned it on. As it logged on to the Internet, she glanced at the ceiling and whispered, "Please, help us."

Once she found the main menu, she looked at the contract.

The words "*we will search until we find your mate*" and "*if you desire children, they should be joyously welcome*" made her uncomfortable. Still, the "*live in luxury*" part stood out. She hadn't eaten a full meal since Dina had passed away. Prices kept going up, four months ago milk cost three dollars for half a gallon, now it was six; fruit was worse, used to three dollars a pound for apples, now it was three dollars each. What was going to be like at the end of the year?

It was the tiny print stating there was no divorce that caused her to balk.

Could she handle it? No man had been close to her since the incident. Would he be gentle with her and help her through it?

Hessie rolled her chair over in the crib. The TV blared that commercial again. She pushed her chair towards her computer. She tapped on "submit" before she changed her mind.

Oh God, oh God.

Both her breathing and her heartbeat sped up. She held a hand to her head, feeling lightheaded and unable to draw a full breath.

What did I just do? Oh Lord. Oh God.

Chapter 2

King Xander Xian's Starship Seeker

Why couldn't their parents have shown a little love and understanding? His big brother, Manier, wouldn't have run away and been brutally murdered if they had shown him some encouragement.

Xander struggled to hold his stomach contents, as the image of his brother's fingers lying next to his hands, the burn marks on his chest, legs and face flashed across his mind.

He slammed his fist into his other hand, shaking his head at how little it helped.

Someone gave a soft, hesitant knock on his door.

"Come in."

Tartar silently moved forward toward Xander; his movements awkward. He tried to hide the brown *sach* in his left hand. Coming to a halt in front of him, he bowed and saluted him.

Xander hid his surprise at Tartar's actions. *Why was he being so formal? And hiding a sach from him?*

Something wasn't right.

He stared pointedly at Tartar's left hand. Then lifted his gaze to his eyes. For the first time in years, Tartar wasn't hiding the swirls of fury in them. Gone was the normal unemotional stone-faced male. He eyed him as he lifted the *sach,* then allowed it to fall to his side. After a momentary hesitation, Tartar held it out toward him.

The hair on the back of his neck stood on end at his friend's demeanor. Not waiting any longer, he snatched the *sach* from him and opened it.

At first glance, his legs gave out on him and had him dropping into his chair like a stone. His body and heart rebelled at what he saw. Mercifully, Tartar shoved the trash can between his legs in time for him to put it to good use.

Before him were pictures of his parents' bodies after being tortured, with their heads occupying a silver tray positioned on the floor near their necks.

Monah... Bormah! Xander's shout was torn from his soul, echoed in his office and beyond. The pictures on the walls rattled, the hanging lights swung and tinkled. No matter how old, no child should see their parents like this.

Sounds of feet running and hands banging on his door filled the room. He couldn't move. Tartar stepped to the door, cracking it. "The prince is fine. He will tell you more when he is ready." Sounds of the retreating warriors faded through the closed door.

The *sach* was still clutched in Xander's hand. He felt something move as it slid from it. He snatched it up in midair before it joined the contents of the trash can.

A data cube.

Carefully, he set it down on his desk as he raised his eyebrow at Tartar.

"It came with the pictures. And I didn't review it."

Xander sat up straight, motioned for Tartar to bring a chair alongside him. He pulled the cube reader out of his side drawer, inserted it, and turned it on. No words were exchanged as they watched.

The first thing they saw was the King of the Coffers, Singe Lin Minor. He was standing, dressed as if he was headed out to conduct state business, leaning against a huge ornate desk.

"Xander Xian, you are an utter failure.

"You couldn't protect your brother, nor your parents. How can you rule a world? Ha! You might win a contest between two soldiers, but you couldn't outwit a feal, our smallest and dumbest animal."

Singe switched his gaze from whomever was recording to the floor at his feet where Xander's parents' bodies lay. He grinned. "It was so much fun playing with these toys. Strange how they cried and screamed but refused to answer my questions. Do you think you could do the same?"

Standing away from his desk, the façade of teasing fell away, leaving his face like granite and eyes spitting fire. "You're next.

"You and anyone or thing you care about. Will be brought down."

Xander wanted to refute everything Singe was saying, but this wasn't a live exchange.

"Be scared. Be terrified. Little 'boy.'"

His raucous laughter filled the room. Then the screen went dark.

Without thinking, they stood, thrusting their chairs back in response. Each had a blaster in one hand and a knife in the other before their seats hit the floor.

Tartar prowled around Xander's office like a feral animal. Xander stood silent. When he realized he had been tricked into showing emotion, he was grateful Singe hadn't witnessed his loss of control. He would have considered him weak. But he'd be wrong. Singe didn't understand how different he was from his family. Xander and Tartar knew each other better than anyone.

They had been friends since infancy. They had shared confidences throughout their lives. Others believe showing emotion is a weakness, Tartar knew was really a strength.

Swiftly, Tartar moved to face him, startling him enough that he took a half step back. He narrowed his eyes as his friend dropped to one knee and bowed his head. Tartar's hands were held out, with his blaster and sword toward Xander. "Sire. My life for yours."

"What? Wait? I'm not..." He wiped his hands down his face. There was no one else. His cousin Vento, from his mother's side, wasn't eligible to take the throne. Only those who had royal blood could rule, and he had none. There was just him.

He wasn't ready, it should be Manier.

A soft voice floated through his mind. *You were always meant to be King. Manier had years in preparation, I did not.*

I never wanted this responsibility, but there was only him now. There is no choice but to be the King. His parents and brother deserved his respect.. He nodded to his friend, extending his arm to him, their hands gripped each other's forearms. He lifted him to his feet. "Tartar, thank you for your oath and your loyalty. May the Gods richly bless you."

Two Kewts Later Aboard the Seeker

"Sire, as your advisor, I must tell you we need to go home. Have your coronation, so you will be recognized as king by all the planets, not just Xandavier."

The generals and senior officers sitting around the conference table watching the tableau unfold before them, nodded. Xander watched them drop their eyes to the floor when they glimpsed the frown on his face. He knew Tartar was right on one level. Xander was amazed no one else joined in his objections.

This was about more than recognizing him as the new King. Something was calling him to go. It was as if he was tied to something and it was drawing him there; at night when he was alone, he felt incomplete. He had to do this... The impression that if he didn't continue this quest, he and his world would be lost. He could physically feel the pull to go there.

"Tartar, you go too far. You may be my advisor, but I must do what I can to find and secure my brother's mate." Xander moved to the port window in jerky movements, his back to everyone else in the room.

He then pivoted to face them all. "I told you when I received Manier's message to come and meet his mate, I was going then. And I'm going now. Be damned whether someone has betrayed us. If they have it doesn't matter where I am, I will be vulnerable.

"Surely you can see I have no choice. Tartar, we must at least try to find her. He would have done the same for me. We can't forget, they will be after her too. Besides, we are a few hurs from the planet he said to meet him on."

He rubbed his face with his hands. "His message didn't tell me much. Just that it was a planet, third from its sun, and its moon had been hit by a giant meteor. The place must be in shambles. I can't leave... abandon her to live in such a wasteland."

He stepped next to the screen covering the front wall of his office, facing his senior officers. "Thank you for your support. You're dismissed. Tartar, a word, please."

The senior officers silently rose and left his office. No one spoke until the last one closed the door on his way out.

He felt his friend's scrutiny. Xander felt like a youngling facing his parents. If he didn't tell them everything, he would not like the consequences. With Tartar it would mean being questioned by Tartar every time they met. He needed his full support. "My friend, please sit. I need to explain something to you, so you can take care of all the security measures."

Xander pointed to a seat directly across from him and smiled when he sat with arms and body open.

"Please, hear me out before you say anything." He coughed and color tinged his cheeks. "I've been listening to a channel from this 'earth' so I can be familiar with their language.... Gods, how many do they have?" He shook his head. "Sorry, I digress. From what I understand, it is called Inglish or English. There are these people who can find your perfect mate in a kewt." The color on his cheeks deepened as he donned a crooked smile.

"I applied."

Tartar's jaw dropped. "Wha? You did what?"

"Now, calm down. I applied." He stood and walked over to a map he had made hanging on his wall. Pointing to a spot on it. "You see this spot? It is the area where Manier's mate is from. If she has a female sibling or she herself applies. It will be the easiest way to find her.

"Plus, you know as well as I do, now I'm going to have to have a mate. The citizens will expect it. And unfortunately, the number of females we are compatible with is growing smaller."

Mouth snapping shut Tartar stiffly sat back. "How long do we have to avoid the Croffers for you to hear from this agency?"

Unable to hide the grin splitting his face. Smiling, something he hadn't been able to do for three *kewts*, "I got a message mins before everyone showed up. They have someone for me to see *todat*."

"What if she isn't your mate?"

"Oh, she is. They sent a vid of her. I'd know her anywhere." Xander handed it to his friend. The ability of their people to recognize their mates by sight giving them an edge in finding a mate. The last time he had been with his parents, they had paraded several females in front of him, hoping he would be drawn to one or two.

I wonder what she is really like. Will she be strong willed like my mother? Will she have to be taught how to walk and talk like a queen?

Tartar interrupted his thoughts, "Sire, may I have a copy of this?"

Xander's dragon stirred in fury. He snatched it out of his hand. Tartar leaned as far back as his chair would let him.

It took Xander a moment to control himself enough to speak. "Why do you need a copy?" His voice wasn't his normal baritone, it was deep and raspy... guttural.

"To show the guards. Sire... are you all right?"

He nodded, handed it back to him, and waved his friend to the door.

As soon as the door closed, he rushed to his private entrance, hidden behind a life-size picture of his parents, to his rooms. He sniffed the air. There was no one there. He tore his clothing off as he dashed to his cleansing room. He needed a cold shower fast.

His body was shifting on its own. He struggled to control it.

Too much tragedy in such a short time. He hadn't had time alone to let his dragon out. Only Tartar and Saarn knew he was a dragon shifter. They had stumbled upon him shortly after he had shifted the first time. He never told his parents or brother they knew, and that they helped him conceal his other half. He had confided in them everything he knew about being a shifter, so if he needed help to deal with any situation that arose, they were there.

They had been a blood pact all those years ago to guard that side of his life. And together, the three of them would find out if the DNA needed to change had been destroyed within the people or pushed to a sort of dormant state. And if it was possible for it to be restored.

He hadn't wanted Tartar to know his dragon was about to surface. Nor how deep his and his dragon's emotional ties were just from seeing her vid. He had to get that side of him back under control.

Hands pressed to the wall he stood under the ice-cold water as it flowed over his body, cooling it, returning him to normal.

He stepped out of the shower, grabbed a drying cloth from the heating bar, and stared at himself. *What would she think of him? His body was firm. He was tall, but not where he towered over everyone.*

Unlike most of his people, his hair was white, hanging down to his shoulders, whereas the majority had dark brown or black hair. Most males wore it long and braided as did the females.

He'd never really paid attention to his battle scars, for once he studied them... would they repel her? He'd heard of females that thought they were ugly and repulsed them.

He shook his head at his own musing and quickly got ready for dinner.

Would she accept him for himself? Would he have to prove himself, like he had with his parents?

Chapter 3

Earth—One Week Later

Bang! Bang!

Whaaaa.

The pounding on the door startled Hessie awake from a sound sleep. The room filled with the baby's cry of fear. Both sounds were bouncing off the walls of the small room. It was so loud, Iona wanted to cover her ears. She had just gotten Hessie to sleep when the pounding on her door jarred her awake.

"Just a minute." She raised her voice over the continuous knocking. She picked up the baby and comforted her. In ten swift steps, she was at the door with the crying infant in her arms. Iona didn't bother to look through the peephole in the door. She yanked it open ready to yell at whoever had woken her niece up, and saw an enormous fist descending toward her face. It stopped less than an inch from the tip of her nose.

A towering figure stood before her. He appeared to be a man, massive, spanning from six and a half to seven feet tall. He'd have to duck to avoid the lintel and twist sideways to squeeze through the door, given his broad shoulders. Her eyes met his, a brilliant emerald green that harkened back to her childhood fascination with a jeweler's window display. His white eyelashes, mirroring his shoulder-length silver-white hair, accentuated their brightness.

She had been ready to yell at him for waking the baby. Instead, when she saw him, she sensed natural authority. He would or could understand a request. Yelling would turn him into an immovable mountain. Deep breath in and out. Calmness was the key. "Hello? How may I help you?"

His glance fell on the crying infant in her arms. He spoke with a slight accent in a soft baritone voice. "Hello, I am looking for Iona Shelby. Are you her?"

Craning her neck to look up, she raised an eyebrow. "Who's asking?" Her hand still clung to the doorknob. It was the only thing holding her in place. His voice made her want to lean into him, not hang on to the door. She had to shake herself mentally to even speak.

"I'm here to escort her to the Dream Makers office, to meet her match."

His voice sent shivers to her core. *What is wrong with me?*

Hessie sniffled and buried her nose in her neck. "How do I know that is where you're from? I thought I'd be getting an email or text notifying me they had found a match for me."

Crap. *Now he knows it's me.*

Just then her laptop went bing. "Excuse me, I need to get that." Leaving the door open, she took one step to her makeshift desk at the counter and checked it. There it was: an email from Dream Makers announcing they had found her match. It had an attachment.

She tapped her foot as she waited for it to download.

Gazing back at him, she said. "It's from them, and they sent a picture of my match."

Then Iona looked at the picture, stiffened, then faced him. "It's you! They said nothing about you coming here to my home. Their letter stated we would meet at the office. A neutral place. This is so not right."

He gave her half bow.

Is he blushing?

A ruddy color tinged his neck to his cheeks.

"You are correct. I beg your forgiveness, but I saw your picture and couldn't wait. I am Xander Xian.

I can take us in my transport, or you can wait for someone else to come."

Xander

As he spoke, he noticed she was swaying toward him like a small tree in a gentle breeze. She was still holding the baby that had quieted down. He pointed at it. "Does the little one come with you? Is she your child?"

He watched her chin come up, her back stiffened, hugged the infant closer. "Yes, she comes with me, and she was my sister's child." Her voice cracked. "She died in an accident, right after her husband had disappeared, so I am responsible for her. She is mine."

He caught the pain in her voice. Was it losing her sister that caused it? The rightness of being here with her swept over him. He studied his brother's female youngling. His mate carried a miracle in her arms, he didn't know how he remained standing. The joy that filled him upon seeing his brother's child made him want to shout to the world about the treasure she was holding.

Gods, what do I know of younglings. He'd never been near any except when he was one himself. All they taught him was how to rule, but that didn't entail caring for something so small. The little one would fit in one hand. So tiny and delicate. *Oh Gods, I need your help.*

It was obvious from her hesitation; she was still unsure of him, probably due to his size... she barely came to his chest in her flats. If she laid the baby down, it was bound to cry again. She was defenseless against him.

Xander stretched out both his hands. "Why are you hesitating? You can see from the email, I am who they have matched you with. We've been alone for a few moments of time, and I haven't attempted to push my way in."

"You're right. We'll come with you. It will take a few minutes to get everything together. I must get Hessie dressed and changed, plus pack the diaper bag." She took a half step back, still holding the door and eyed him up and down. A moment later her hand pulled the door open wider. "It would be better if you come in."

Xander ducked his head when he entered. He noticed out of the corner of her eye; she kept glancing at him. One step and he was in the center of the room. No wonder she was nervous about him being there. He took up almost all the space in her tiny dwelling. He stayed silent, letting his senses absorb every nuance of her home.

Surveying the room, it hit him was how tiny their whole dwelling was. It would fit in his clensing room. The emotion she had toward the infant filled every nook and cranny. It wasn't from any heater, atmosphere in the room. Everything was placed with care and thoughtfulness. All the furniture was well used, but taken care of, just as the child was. Not from duty, but with a heart full of love.

He craved emotional support, not the material gifts his parents always gave. They made friends for him based on status, not mutual support. Yet, over time, his training comrades, like Tartar, his main advisor, and Saar, the military commander, became his true friends. They'd grown up together, relying on each other. A deep bond tied them together.

No one who ever visited the family's private rooms would have sensed the love between his parents toward Manier and him. It was just as sterile as a medical room.

When he lost any of his warriors, he mourned deeply. It hurt him to know their families suffered such a loss. Even his own rooms didn't show his emotions. But here, this was a new, distinct experience. He could now identify what he'd always wanted but had never been able to put it into words. Anyone who entered this dwelling for any length of time would sense the emotions that filled it on all levels. They would know the experience of being loved by someone who would willingly sacrifice everything for them.

Something he had dreamed of having all his life.

His eyes tracked Iona to the corner bed. She quickly changed the sleeping child's clothes, then moved to a white box, pulling out bottles and outfits. After donning her jacket, she swaddled the baby, slung the bag over her shoulder, lifted the child, and faced him.

"We're ready."

She had done all that in less than five minutes. Nodding, he opened the door. As they approached it, she stopped. "Would you mind getting my key out of my coat pocket on my right side? If I try to get it, I might wake her. And she really needs this nap."

Slowly and gently, using only three of his fingers, he felt for her keys and pulled them out. When they left her apartment, he locked the door, raised an eyebrow at her, and she put her right hip forward for him to put the key back in her pocket.

Halfway down the hall toward the stairwell, he stopped, moving in front of her. "Would you like me to carry the bag for you? I would offer to carry the little one, but I've never held one before and don't want to harm her."

In answer, her shoulder slump and the bag slid off. He caught it before it hit the floor and smiled at her. When they reached the stairs, he motioned for her to let him go first. "In case you fall, it will be better for you and the child to fall into me than the metal."

"Thank you."

When they reached the street, he saw a strange look on her face as she glanced toward the men standing in a group. Xander's hand dropped to his side as he walked up to the biggest guy, that appeared to be waiting for him. "Any problems?"

"No. No, sir. Everything is just as you left it,"

He noticed her face went blank the moment she saw him shake hands with Arnie. He thought he heard her sniff the air. Her eyes sharpened when Arnie answered him with a tremor in his voice.

"That's good. I will pass on an excellent report to Simon. I have one other job for you... if you are interested."

"Yes, of course. Whatever you want."

Xander looked deeply into his eyes. "If you see anyone hassling this female or her child, you contact me, then rush to aide her. She is always to be safe and unharmed."

Swallowing and nodding so fast, he looked like a bobble-headed doll. "Yes. No harm to her or hers. Contact me if someone hassles them."

"That's right. Guard them with your life. Because we will take your life and the lives of anyone else you care about, if you don't."

Then the man stepped in front of Iona, opened the car door for her and Hessie, and he stepped backward, keeping a distance between them. Xander nodded at his actions.

Xander helped into the vehicle, closed her door, and walked around to the driver's side and got in.

She gazed at him silently.

He waved at the man as he pulled out onto the road, then glanced at her.

"You're upset? Did I do something wrong?"

"I trying to process everything that just happened, is all."

"Is something unusual about what happened?"

"Well, to begin with, there are normally several gang members waiting at the bottom of the stairs to hassle us. Then there is the big guy you were talking to. I know him as Arnie. He's one of the meanest ones around. The worst of the worst. He has killed men and women who spoke to him like you did. When he killed them, it was after he tortured them first. From what my neighbors say he likes to inflict pain.

And you had him taking care of your car. You scared him; I mean, really terrified him. Then the mention of this 'Simon' upped his fear even more. And the last thing is, why did you order him to protect Hessie and me, and to report to you? Then threaten to kill him and his family. What am I to you? We just met. We have decided nothing." By the time they finished talking, she was whisper-shouting at him.

"I'm sorry if I've upset you. But when I arrived, I saw the males and knew they were waiting for an excuse to make trouble. After finding out who their boss was, I made a deal with him... that was the Simon I mentioned. Then I hired Arnie to watch my transport. I thought if he did what he said, someday I might have a reason to need his help."

Turning his head, he looked at Iona and let his gaze sweep down and encompass Hessie, too. "As for why I would tell him to protect you and the young one. I would like to hold this discussion until we are at the Dream Mates' offices. I have some things I need to show you, and they are there."

"All right. But if I don't like the answers, I want you to take us home."

Chapter 4

Dream Makers Inc.

It was so hard to wait for him to come and open her door. She knew she could have opened it, but getting out of the car while carrying a baby would have created an enormous problem. So, she waited. Once he opened it, she gazed up at him. "Please take her so I can get out?"

His eyes widened, and he hesitated.

Holding his hand open, his facial expression was comical. He examined his hands then stared at Hessie aghast.

She could tell he was about to say, "No," so instead of saying anything, she held the baby out, and he automatically extended his hands. She laid her in his palms. Fear filled his eyes. She let a giggle escape until terror flashed across his face. She had run into large men, not as large as he was, but big. They were so afraid they would hurt a puppy or kitten because of their size, when, in fact, they were gentler with them than their smaller counterparts.

After climbing out of the car, she had mercy on Xander and took the infant while he got the diaper bag, slung it over his shoulder and then guided her through the entrance of The Dream Makers Inc building.

As they entered the main lobby, the smell of flowers surrounded her. A desk was centered behind a long counter. Seeing us, the tall woman sitting behind it stood, made her way over to us, in three-inch heels clicking on the marble floor. She halted in front of them.

She bowed slightly. "Xiansah, you found her. We have set aside the second room on the right for you. Refreshments and a crib, as you requested have been prepared for you." She remained standing until they had walked past her toward the room to her right.

Iona glanced up at him. "I thought you said your last name was Xian... not Xiansah."

"It is. She added my title at the end,"

"Title? Like Mister?"

"No... I'll answer your question in just a moment, can you wait till we can sit down?"

She nodded as he stopped and opened the door to a room the smell of fresh bread, roasted meats, apples and oranges washed over her. They were all laid out on an enormous boardroom type table and a crib had been placed in the corner. Iona slammed to a halt so quickly he bumped into her, knocking her about a foot forward, then catching her by the arms to keep her from falling. "Are you okay?"

"Yes, I- I- I couldn't believe my eyes! I've never seen this much food in my life." She waved her hand at the display on the table, shaking her head at the waste. She walked past the conference room table ladened with food to the crib set up in the corner, and laid Hessie down.

Xander trailed her, placed the bag by the side, and led her towards the sunlit window on the other side. She halted, peering out at the street where clusters of people, thirty or more, dodged each other like cars. The aroma of food wafting in redirected her attention back to the table.

Iona

"Are you going to tell me about the name she called you?"

Iona paused next to the chair he pulled out for her near the head of the table and sat down.

"Yes, I am." He took the seat next to hers. "It's part of what we need to speak about." Picking up the folder sitting in front of him, he pulled it closer.

"Another is this." He angled it so they both could see what was in it.

Iona saw a picture of her sister Dina laughing up at a man that looked very similar to Xander. She raised a questioning eye at him. "He looks like you. Who is he?"

"He was my older brother, Manier. He was killed four months ago. Does he look familiar at all?"

"No." Iona paused, narrowing her eyes at him. "Why would I recognize him?"

"I had hoped you had met him." He pointed to the picture of Dina and Manier laughing, then turned the page and showed a very pregnant Dina shopping with him in the baby department of a store, their cart loaded with things.

Her gaze went from him to the picture.... her eyes filled with tears at how happy they were. "Are you saying Manier was Dina's husband and Hessie's father?" The sensation of panic-pain sitting on her chest had her struggling to keep her breathing even. She hadn't survived, but her baby had. And she was Iona's baby, now. There had been no one to question whose child she was. In her heart and mind, Hessie was her child.

Iona stood up so she could look down at his face. Struggling to stand and not run, her whole body vibrated as tight as a bowstring on a violin. "Is this where you rip her from me? I mean really, are you here to take Hessie from me? If you think you're going to get away with it... I'll fight you. No man's name is on her birth certificate. Dina never told me her married name or her husband's name. She only told me to name her Hester."

"Please, sit down. I am here because we are a match. This company has done the research and matched us. And I know you are my life-mate. Just as I've realized, your sister was my brother's. I want to help you and have you as my mate. But first I need to tell you about my brother and how all this happened. Will you sit down and listen?" His voice was soft and pleading.

She moved back to the table. And stood by her chair.

"While I talk, would you like something to eat or drink? I believe the little one will wake soon, and it would be better to have eaten before she does so."

She searched his face and saw his sincerity. "Thank you, I will." The two filled their plates from the food spread out before them, and Xander brought a carafe of coffee and another of water to their seats.

"Manier was four years older than I. Our Bormah and Monah, I believe you call them father and mother, were the King and Queen of Xandavier. My brother was the Crown Prince, the next in line to rule, so his requirements were much more than my own. We were the future leaders of our world, he told us we had to be better than anyone else, if one person had a higher score in anything, we were considered a failure. Our punishment was swift and brutal.

"One day Manier had enough. He told Bormah to give the crown to me. Then one day, Manier disappeared. We've been searching for him for years."

Pointing to her plate with his fork, he urged her to eat. "When your moon got hit by the asteroid, and your earth was impacted by it, other species discovered its existence. I hoped we would find him here."

Xander paused and pinched the bridge of his nose. "Then I received a message from him. He told me the coordinates and to come meet his Life-Mate."

He stopped speaking when Iona jumped to her feet, shaking her head, and edging away from him toward Hessie as if she was going to grab her and run.

Moving swifter than his size denoted, he quickly blocked her, put his arms around her shoulder, "I'm sorry. I know this is a shock to you, but I am not human, and Hessie is only half. Please sit down and listen. Don't be rash. We have little time."

She shook her head and whispered. "What...? Not human? Xandavier? Where? Other... species? No time? What...."

This isn't happening. It's all a dream. I'll wake up and everything will be back to normal. She closed her eyes, rubbed them with her hands, and opened them. *Nothing changed. It wasn't a dream; it was a nightmare.*

Weeping, she hit him on his chest while he wrapped her in his arms.

"Iona, please. I'm not trying to take her from you. We really are a perfect match, and it gives us a solution. You know Hessie can't live here. When she grows up and people realize she isn't like them, she's going to have problems." His hands cupped her shoulders, easing her slightly away from his chest.

Gazing up at him. Xander continued. "This is not the way I wanted to do this. I wanted us to have more time together. But my enemies and those of our people know where we are—they're coming. If they find Hessie, they won't hesitate to take her. She is the next in line to rule. The only protection she will have requires us to join. Be my mate, and Hessie will always be yours."

Examining his face, she could see every emotion he was feeling, he held nothing back. He hadn't lied to her or tried to force her to do anything against her will. Casting her gaze at the pictures on the table and back to Hessie. The extra small print in the contract niggled at her mind — they wouldn't stop looking for a mate for her.

This "man" had done nothing wrong to her or set her alarms off. Something about him pulled her towards him. The sound of his voice reached something within her no one had ever touched. Was she willing to grab a chance at happiness for her and Hessie?

Stiffening, Iona stood tall in the circle of his embrace. Her arms at side with hands fisted, and her chin lifted. "Yes. Yes, we'll go with you. I'll be your mate."

Click! Click!

"Highness, we need to go now." A gruff male voice filled the room.

"That was Tartar. He wouldn't interrupt us unless the Croffers were closer than I thought." He turned her around to guide her to Hessie and picked up the diaper bag. "Pickup Hessie and anything else you want to take with us. Then stand right in front of me with your back towards me."

The tone and tension in his voice told her he was serious. She glanced around the room, Hessie in her arms. Obeying his directive, she literally bumped her back into his chest, felt the diaper back pushed back behind him as his arms locked around her, holding them tightly like a belt in a carnival ride.

"Now."

Chapter 5

Space and Beyond

B rilliant light flickered in front of her eyes, blinding her. Grateful that Hessie was asleep, she bent her head over her and closed her eyes. She shivered at the pressure she felt in her ears. Xian's powerful arms assured her he wouldn't let go. It had been so long since she had someone to depend on.

What? Where did a sense of comfort and strength in Xander's arms come from? Even though she and Dina had become close, she was still her sister, not a parent or a lover. She hadn't had that since her parents died when she was fourteen.

Oh Lord. Did I take us from the pot to the fire? Were things really falling apart instead of coming together?

Hessie chose that moment to snuggle closer.

He asked, and she had said "yes." Now here she and Hessie were in Xander's arms, being transported somewhere. And she was going to be a queen. Her—a nobody from nowhere, very little education because of the world she lived in. Never in her wildest dreams would she have thought this would happen to her. She wasn't qualified to be a queen. She could barely handle Hessie and the decisions for her. Much less for an entire world. And she had no clue how to dress or act like one.

God, what have I done?

The flashing lights through her eyelids stopped, her ears weren't feeling any pressure, her stomach had returned to its normal position, and the deep breath she took was full of sweet clean air, unlike anything she'd ever experienced. She felt a slight squeeze from his arms. She opened her eyes.

They were in a glass room inside a larger room. A quick survey didn't reveal a door, but she could see there were two other places like where they stood, each with a stand. They resembled a music stand, each with a tablet or monitor on it.

Xander was still holding them. Tilting her face, she stared at him till he looked down at her. She opened her mouth. He gently lifted her chin with his finger to close it as the glass filled with a white smoke, then blue. She waved her hand in front of them to get the mist away from Hessie when the smoke dissipated, and the glass walls lifted into the ceiling.

"The mist doesn't taste pleasant. And I didn't have time to warn you before we left earth."

Iona gently separated herself from him. "What was that misty thing? I hope it won't hurt Hessie at this age."

Xander cupped her elbow to steer her out of the area they were in. "No, it should have no effect on her or you. It is simply a type of disinfectant. It strips out of our body anything that could bring harm to the ship or the crew."

She attempted to act like herself. How could she, though? She'd never been on a ship... a spaceship. No one had ever taken her elbow—my hand, yes, but not an elbow. It brought back romance stories from ancient times. They called it genteel manners. Iona suspected if she made a move to leave his side, it might become a painful hold rather than a light touch.

Letting him guide her, she took her time ogling everything. It was so strange from Earth, so different from what she thought it would be. It has automatic lighting, for goodness' sake. Nothing was out of place. Whereas poor broken down Earth nothing was spotlessly clean in common areas. Here, she thought she could eat off the floor. It seemed a safe place to lay

Hessie even. Cleaner than most restroom baby areas, that's for sure.

They strolled down a hallway, its bare beige walls and the dark metal floor stretching into the darkness ahead. However, the darkness always retreated. Every three steps, lights illuminated their path while the ones behind extinguished. She marveled at this, feeling like a first-time visitor to a big city, unable to hold back her exclamations of wonder. A sudden urge made her look up at Xander, who was smiling at her reaction.

Lord, hope he doesn't think I'm stupid.

They turned a corner to find a set of double doors that opened as they approached. She recognized what it was immediately. It was a medical facility of some type. It had the curtained cubicles, beds, medical equipment, and self-locking cabinets, she knew normally contained highly addictive drugs. She wanted to ask but after catching his smile from her reaction; she didn't to remove any doubt she was a country bumpkin.

He squeezed her elbow to bring them to a halt. He didn't have to ask for help. Four men in yellow uniforms came rushing over. One had an orange cap on and lapels on his outfit.

"Sire, how can we help you?"

Iona caught him staring at Hessie. She pulled her blanket up over her head and snuggled her closer.

As if everything was normal Xander moved his hand from her elbow to her waist. It was as if he was making a statement of some kind.

"Alain. Iona, let me introduce you to Royal Healer Alain S'tryker. He is head of all Healers and medics for the Royal family. He will attend to you and Hester. Alain, this is my mate, your Queen, Iona, and our daughter Hester."

Why didn't he tell him Hessie was Manier and Dina's little one? Maybe he thought this Alain was as creepy as she did. She didn't like the avid gleam in Alain's eyes when they fell on Hessie or her.

The Healer Alain bowed so low she was afraid he'd hit his head on the floor. "Queen Iona, Princess Hester. Come this way so I can examine you and get your DNA in the database."

Iona planted her feet at his first words. Xander's arm urged her to follow Alain. Her feet skidded a little on the floor. Her gaze was focused on his face when he tilted his head down with an eyebrow lifted. "May I speak with you privately?"

Nodding, he ignored the healer, and guided her into a room with a door and a window with blinds. Inside, he shut and locked the door, then let down the blinds. "Is this private enough?"

"Yes, thank you." She paced in front of an unmade bed shoved against the wall.

He didn't say a word. She felt the air move slightly and glanced around. He had moved to the wall and propped himself up against it, his attention centered on her.

She inspected the bed, laid Hessie on it, stood next to it with her hand on Hessie, and faced Xander. "I don't know how to say this nicely, so I'm just going to say it."

He slowly nodded his head.

"I... that Alain, the Healer? I don't like him at all. He gave me the creeps... hee-bee-jee-bees. Understand?"

"You're saying you just met a male, and you don't like him? He made you uncomfortable. Yes?"

"Yes. I felt like slime was dripping off him. And I don't want him touching me or Hessie. I don't trust him." It was so hard to stand firm when she was trembling like a leaf in a windstorm inside.

"Hmm. This could be a problem. You both need to be examined. It is ship policy. But if you don't trust him...."

"Isn't there anyone else, someone older? We could, see?"

"I do have my old physician on ship. He just retired and wanted to go on one more mission with me. He hoped Manier would be alive."

"Could... would you send for him?" She smiled at him.

"He's down the hallway giving a class to some Healers on who knows what. I'll go get him. You and Hessie stay here. It will only take me a few minutes."

Iona checked on Hessie. She hadn't moved since she laid her on the bed, stepped to Xander's side and touched his arm. He was three feet from the door and stopped the instant her hand landed on his jacket. She stretched up and kissed him on his jaw. "Thank you so much for understanding."

He had the oddest expression, eyes half lidded, cheeks taut. His mouth was open slightly. What had caused that?

He gave her a short, stiff bow and left.

He had left the door ajar, so she closed it softly and stepped back to the bed.

She was about to open the blinds when there was a loud commotion outside her room. The loud clanging of a metal bowl or cups dropping to the floor woke Hessie. She started with a little whimper, then a full-blown cry. That cry meant a diaper change was needed. Then she'd want her bottle. Iona searched for the diaper bag.

No bag. Think. Xander wasn't carrying when he left. Oh no! It had to be the team that took everything when they were in decontamination. Until they got that bag, it would not be fun around Hessie. She would be relentless until she either got naked or her nappy was changed.

With Hessie hiccup-crying in her arms, she turned toward door as it opened. Expecting Xander, she gasped at the man standing in front of her. He wasn't in yellow. He was in a deep gray suit of armor that fit like skin. The grin on his face made her think of the gang in her neighborhood, but worse.

Evil. Pure evil.

She said nothing; she went between the bed and the wall with Hessie in her arms.

There was no other place to go. She couldn't get to the door. He filled it.

He took a step toward her, and she screamed with all the volume she had, "Fire! Fire!"

If it weren't so serious she would have laughed at his expression. Fear flashed across his face, then he glanced around. Nothing was burning. He stared at her, his face lit up, like that of a cat playing with a mouse. "So, you want to play?"

Holding Hester as securely as she could, she moved her body from left to right, hoping he would try to figure out which way she was going to run. While moving side-to-side, she slowly eased the blanket off Hessie but held it to the infant as if it was still wrapped around her. While her self-defense instructor, Manny, was speaking, she heard him say repeatedly: "keep your focus on their eyes." The eyes would telegraph their movements.

As soon as she noticed his eye twitch on the left side, she quickly dashed to the right and threw Hessie's blanket in his face, screaming, "Fire!"

Chapter 6

Which Royal Healer?

Pulling his old Healer Ranin Soldar away from all his adoring students was taking more time than Xander wanted. They were finally free of them and had taken two steps out of the classroom when he heard the scream.

"Fire."

It wasn't the scream it was the voice that put fear in his heart—it was Iona's. She was in danger. She and Hester. It baffled him as he ran to Iona. Why was everyone else but Ranin running away? You didn't run from fire; you went to put it out with whatever you could grab on the way.

He was twenty feet away when she screamed again and was running out the door with the baby in her arms and a warrior chasing her, with Hester's blanket covering half of his face and chest. The warrior yanked it off himself, tossing it to the floor.

Xander recognized him immediately. He was supposed to be in security under heavy guard. He had killed and raped a young female on the planet they had just left.

How the Helos did he get out? And why had he come here? If he hurts a hair on her head, he's dead. My Gods! I haven't even kissed her and the thought of someone harming her makes me want to kill them...

Two more strides and Xander would have them safe. He slammed into the escaped prisoner as his filthy hands touched Iona's shoulder. Iona went spinning into the wall, slamming her back, then sliding down to sit on the floor, hanging on to a crying Hessie.

Xander picked up the fugitive and hit him one time. He went flying into the room he had left, banged his head on the bed, and collapsed on the floor.

Securing the door with a chair under the knob, Xander commed security to get a team there and to cancel the fire alert.

Xander, afraid of what he'd see, twisted to face Iona and Hessie. They were being tenderly cared for by Ranin. Iona was smiling at him and letting him touch Hessie.

He went to her side and lifted her up and carried her while Hessie clung to her as they entered the neighboring cubicle. Setting them both on the bed. Ranin pulled the curtains as she laid back with Hessie on her chest.

Impatient to ensure they were alright, Xander refused to leave her side.

Alain entered with four medics and went immediately to him, ignoring Iona and Hessie.

He gritted his teeth and stepped away from Alain's hands. "I'm fine. Leave me alone. It's the baby and my Queen that might be hurt." He sharply stepped around Alain and his entourage and planted himself opposite Ranin, at Iona's side.

Words failed him. If spoken, his words would lash Alain like a whip on a condemned prisoner. He yearned to purge this unprecedented fury, directed at anyone threatening his mate. He sensed his body's heat dissipate. The thought of harm to her or the baby would have driven him to become a berserker – relentless, uncontrollable. He raised his trembling hand behind Iona's back. As his focus intensified, the shaking gradually subsided until it ceased completely.

When he tilted his head to see what was happening between Ranin and his mate, his gaze was snared by the baby's eyes. They were his brother's, brilliant blue with flecks of silver in them. What he saw in them made him catch his breath and hold it. She was sending waves of comfort to him and those around her. This six-month-old infant was doing what took years to learn.

The tension in Medical was drained and replaced with a sense of peace and comfort. She pulled her thumb out of her mouth and smiled at him, blinked, and fell asleep.

Xander lifted his eyes to find Iona and Ranin chatting softly. She lifted her head and turned her face directly to his, her mouth slightly ajar. He bent toward her... his focus completely on her full damp lips. Without thought, his whole being curled towards her, just a few more inches, and he'd have his prize.

"Highness. Please, we must check you over." Ranin's jarring voice came from behind him.

"I am unharmed. Check on the prisoner." Xande's voice was crusty. "I hit him hard." When had Alain been centered on him before? He'd never seemed like a pompous fool. Was it because he was no longer Ranin's assistant? Had he always been so narcissistic? Had his title gone to his head?

Ranin turned off the screens over Iona and Hester. "Sire, both are in good shape. No harm came to either. However, your Queen has been cutting back on her food, so you need to see that she eats more. Your daughter is happy and healthy, which is all one can ask for in such a tiny one."

A smile appeared on Iona's face; she flexed her fingers in spots on Hessie's side, waking her. Giggles burst from the baby as Iona's fingers light touched her in the same areas. The flicker of her eyelids told Xander she knew exactly what she was doing, and she had been keeping track of him as he dealt with her attacker and Alain. He plucked Hessie off her chest, grasped her to his chest with one hand. He offered the other to her, assisting her to sit up.

She smiled her thanks, motioning with her free hand toward Ranin. "Is this the Healer, you told me about?"

"Yes." He bowed slightly to the older male. "Iona, this is, or was, my Royal Healer Ranin Soldar. He had charge of me since I was Hester's age. Which is why he is now retiring. Before me, he had charge of my brother, my parents, and their parents."

He lifted his hand toward Iona and the baby. "Healer Soldar, this is my mate and queen, Iona, and our daughter Hester."

Healer Soldar bowed deeply, "My honor, your Highness."

Her eyes went to Xander in question. All he did was nod and arch an eyebrow. She cleared her throat. "Healer Soldar, I know I, uh, we have just met." She bit her bottom lip. "Would you consider not retiring? Instead, might you serve as my and Hester's Royal Healer?"

He was silent.

"Please?"

Alain burst into the room, out of breath from running across Medical. "What's going on here? I'm the Royal Healer." His gaze went from the King to Soldar. "My assistant said you were asking him to be your healer. I am your healer."

Hester, in Xander's arm, shrunk back from him. He was totally surprised when Iona jumped off the bed and stood in front of him, Hester and Ranin, with her arms spread wide. "You are not my healer. Nor will you be Hester's. I will not let you touch either of us. In fact, I don't want you knowing anything about us."

Xander was so proud of her. Other things were at play here that he hadn't talked with her about. He placed a comforting hand on her shoulder. And was surprised she slowly lowered her arms.

Hester's cooing could be heard throughout their area. Iona let her arms rest at her side. She turned to her right, put her hand on Ranin, drawing him to her side. Xander wasn't shocked at all when she announced. "He is our healer."

Like a petulant boy, Alain took a step closer to him, and Hester's eyes widened, letting loose a scream Xander thought would break everyone's eardrums.

Ranin stepped around everyone who was stunned by the amount of noise coming out of something so small. He pulled Hester from his arm. As he crooned an old Xian nursery song, the screams got softer and softer until she fell silent. Asleep in his arms.

Xander stared at Alain. "I believe she has picked her healer." When Alain opened his mouth to protest, Xander held up a hand. "Do you really want her to scream like that again?"

Alain's eyes burned with fury. He closed them. When he opened them, there was no emotion reflected as he walked off with his assistants.

Ranin nodded after them. "Sire, you have made an enemy. Be careful."

"I know." He ran a hand down his face.

"Do you need to do any tests for Iona and Hester?"

"No, I took care of them while you were defending us."

"I'm taking my family to our rooms. Thank you, my friend. I know she would never have let him examine either of them."

Iona

Wow. What a day. Met her future husband, some married to him, Hester was now her daughter. And she was a Queen. She met two scumbags. One said he was her doctor with eyes that undressed her and looked at Hessie as if she was the newest thing to use as a science project. No way. How had she stood up like that to him? She'd never done anything like that before.

And the man who attacked her and Hester. She'd seen his eyes. He wasn't insane; he knew exactly what he was doing. His focus centered on her. She had sensed her death at his hands was the only way he would be satisfied. This was no chance encounter. Why, and who would do this?

It was the third time today Xander had protected her from another man. The first two times were the neighborhood bully and Alain.

She was so ready for a nap, her stomach felt hollow. What she needed was food, then rest for both her and Hessie. Her thoughts were broken into when he grabbed her hand and took them out of Medical. She followed him like a tired child. They passed several closed doors, and men walking down the hallways. Then on an elevator and up. They went up so fast her stomach was in her shoes when they stopped, and the doors opened. Xander lifted her chin. "This is the senior officer's quarters floor, #31. Our quarters are the only ones without a number on or near the door."

They stepped towards the hallway to the right. Counting to herself she was stopped in front of the fourth door, she had counted. A glance down the hallway, both ways. Everything was identical. Same color of beige. The floor was beige with brown spots. Silver metal struts or bars of some kinds connected the beige panel. There was nothing to show how to open any door. When they'd stopped in front of their door, a light shone down from over their heads. She tilted her head, then Xander's big hand gently pushed it down.

Woosh the door disappeared upward. Iona could feel the smile form on her face. As she watched it lift like a curtain on stage.

She heard Xander speaking. All she heard was "wawa wawa wan."

Her vision blurred as she focused on his actions. She placed Hester in a crib, identical to her old one. Panic bubbled up. She didn't have the strength to say anything. Her body swayed like a sapling in a windstorm. The vertigo was worse than when she got off a merry-go-round. The room wouldn't stay still. It increased in speed. Black dots floated in front of her as her legs turned to rubber and collapsed.

What's happening to me?

Chapter 7

Iona—Two days later.

What? Hessie, she's crying. I need to feed her. So tired and so warm and comfortable. Hessie...

Then I remembered that deep voice. "Hessie is fine. She's been changed and fed. Sleep, love. Sleep. You're not alone anymore." I trusted it. I let my worry and fears evaporate.

Third Dat

Hot. Too hot, too many covers. She rubbed her face on her pillow. But it didn't give or scrunch. It was hot. Who ever heard of a pillow that was hot?

Her head felt like it weighed a ton. It was so hard to lift it up.

Squinting, she focused on different objects around her. She was in a bed... above her head seemed to be the headboard of a bed. It was bigger than anything she'd ever seen. It was taller than she was and at five foot nine, that was tall for a woman. There were pictures on the wall, nothing she'd ever seen. There was a group of immense chairs and a table in one corner. Across from it was a baby crib.

Iona lunged up. She had to get to Hessie. She remembered her crying but not getting up and taking care of her. Only that deep voice telling her to sleep. She hadn't wanted to sleep. Lord. She could feel heat in her face. Even without a mirror, she knew she was blushing. No, she had told the voice she wanted him, not sleep. He was hers, and she was his.

Her pillow moved. Now her face was on fire. It was Xander. She felt a cool breeze on her skin, looking down. Oh, no! Naked. She snatched the covers up to cover herself. She'd never been naked in front of anyone but their doctor.

Sneaking a glance at him, with the blankets bunched around his hips, she couldn't tell if he was in the same condition as her or not.

His sexy voice, the one that aroused her so much was saying something. "Good morning, mate. I am so sorry. We had no knowledge that the first time we went into warp-drive it could affect humans so severely."

His eyes caught hers. "You've been asleep for three days. What would you like first, shower or food?"

"I... I've been asleep for three days?" She squeaked, then cleared her throat. "Water. I would like water first, and where is Hessie?"

"Hessie is fine. She is with Ranin and two of my finest men that have small siblings. She likes them both. In fact, she picked them out. We lined them up for me to interview and she crawled over to each one, pulled herself up by hugging their legs. The others tried to interact with her, and she screamed so loud... needless to say, we lumped them in with males she doesn't care for."

She guzzled the glass of water he had given her as he expounded on Hessie's actions. Snorted water up her nose as she pictured Hessie screaming with the other men as she tried to smother her laughter. Coughing, she felt a hand almost the size of her back, gently patting her like she did the baby to get it to burp.

She put out a hand to stop him to stop him. "I'm okay. I'm okay."

"You haven't told me where she is? Or what happened to me? Did it affect her?"

"She is in a connecting room to the living room with Baston and Calife. I've been taking care of her during the night. And Ranin has been checking on all of us throughout. He said she was unaffected because she had all the nutrients she needed and was part Xian. You, on the other hand, had been starving yourself, were exhausted, and fully human."

"Oh." Iona ran her hands through her hair. "I need a shower and then food." She twisted toward the side of the bed closest to her, dragging the bedcovers with her. She looked over her shoulder back at him. "Is there anything else I should know?"

"I don't think so. You don't need to be shy with me. We are married, and I have seen all of you."

She thought she saw a twinkle in his eyes and sensed he was chuckling inside. "Point me to the bathroom. Does it work like stuff on earth?"

"I'll go with you." He twisted and put his bare legs over the side, grabbed a robe, and put it on. "I'll cover up to ease your fears."

As he got up, his rear was clear to see as his back muscles flexed, putting on the robe. Heat flowed over and through her at the sight. She wanted him. When he faced her again, he was fastening his robe, and his chest pec muscles were visible as they flexed when he moved. The need to reach out and touch him was overwhelming, something she couldn't control.

He ripped the covers from the foot of the bed and tossed one to her. "There, now you have a robe, too."

She caught her reflection in the mirror. Wrapped in a green blanket, her face beet red, her dark hair showed red highlights. And for the first time since Dina died, she felt alive. Really alive.

Xander stopped at the foot of the bed, held his hand out to her. She clasped it and walked with him into the bathroom. He led her around from the sink to each item, including laundry and fresh towels, ending up in the shower. He never mentioned her turning pink each time she looked at him. She had relaxed in their state of undress when he explained how to work the shower. Then dropped his robe to the floor. "I think I'll join you in the shower. Your color keeps changing and you tremble at times. I'm worried you'll fall and hurt yourself."

Xander acknowledged the luck he had in selecting his mission team. Each member was not only highly intelligent and resourceful but also adept at deploying both intellect and brawn to accomplish their tasks. They thrived on unpredictability, using surprise as a key strategy. When Xander instructed Benson to resume work and Buel to clean up, Buel's understanding gaze confirmed his personal responsibility for the protective action.

His chest brushed against Iona's back, and her nipples hardened to pinpoints. They hurt and hungered for him. She bit the inside of her cheek to keep from begging him to ease her pain. Closing my eyes, she smelled him. It reminded her of a fresh breeze from the ocean. There was another fragrance too.... Lemons her mother used to make lemonade with. These were her two favorite smells.

Xander's deep voice came over her in waves. "Turn around and hold on to me. I won't let you fall, and I won't do anything but wash you like I would Hester. Trust me."

Lord, didn't he realize it wasn't him? It was herself she didn't trust.

As she turned toward him, she felt a rush of excitement and nervousness coursing through her veins. "I'm going to wash your hair first, and finish with your feet. Before I touch you anywhere, I'll tell you, so just relax. Lean on me. I won't let you fall."

It felt divine to have him wash her hair.

He scratched her scalp as he massaged her head, then stroked her like a cat as he rinsed the shampoo out. True to his word he didn't make any comments about her state of arousal, only what he was doing.

I didn't open my eyes. I felt his hardness brush up against her. Each time she shivered, he asked me if I was okay. All she could do was nod.

When he got to her center, he lightly ran the washcloth through her legs, easing it first through her buttocks to her dripping entrance and up to her nub. One touch and her legs gave out. She had never felt like this before. The only time she had allowed anyone to touch her was in high school. All the girls were bragging about how wonderful it felt. And now they were women, not girls. They said it hurt at first. They hadn't lied about that part.

Now she knew why. This is how she should have felt when he touched her. She should have hungered for "it." Not to be part of the "in crowd." The pain and humiliation had been for naught. She could never bring myself to tell them.

True to his word Xander caught her before she hit the floor and sat her down on a bench in the back of the shower. He washed her as if she were totally helpless. Then he opened the door and grabbed a warm towel from a drawer next to it.

He bundled her up in it, not bothering to dry himself. Then held her in his arms, placed her on the bed, and tucked her in. Dripping over the carpet and floor, and climbing in next to her, he wrapped his arms around her.

She couldn't stop herself. She buried her face in the curve of his shoulder. Her self-control was gone. Iona reached out with her tongue and licked the water droplets from his upper chest, lapping them up from his shoulder to his stomach.

"Iona, I won't be able to be like I was in the shower if you continue. My body wants you badly. I need to touch you, suckle at your breast, bury my tongue in your slit, then nibble on your nub before I join my body with yours. Attuning physical union like my heart is attuned to yours."

Without a word, she rolled onto my back, gripped his ears, drew his mouth to her breast. As soon as she felt the wetness and his tongue curling around, and a gentle sucking, I couldn't be silent any longer.

"Please more. Harder."

As she spoke, Xander had slipped one arm around her back to her breast. He caressed and plucked at her breast, *imitating* his mouth devouring the other one. She guided his free hand down to her center. "Please, I need you."

Tears running down the side of her face into her hair and ears. Her body trembled and her hips tilted upward toward him, trying to guide him to a deeper touch.

His leg separated hers. She felt his straining cock on her thigh. It left a wetness her body needed inside her. She reached down his front and caressed him. "I need you now. I hurt. Take the hurt away."

It was as if she pulled the pin on a grenade. Everything happened within seconds. Using his thighs, he pushed her legs further apart as he whispered in her ear. "I wanted to taste you, but I can't let you hurt, either."

He nibbled on her neck as he slowly pushed into her center. He leaned on one arm by her shoulders. Letting his lips caress the tender skin by her ears. His chest brushed hers, teasing her nipples, making them long for his lips. With his other hand, he slipped it between them, down to her nub. He wasn't hurting her, but he wasn't really in her, either. And she needed him. When he touched her nubbin, her body frantically followed its movement.

He lifted slightly. Both her hands were free, and she cupped his butt. When he moved toward her core, she thrust up and pulled him toward her, until she was full. It hurt, but it soothed the other hurt.

"You shouldn't have done that. I didn't want to hurt you."

"Xander, it didn't hurt. I needed you, and you were taking too long."

He lifted his head. Their eyes met. She knew he saw the truth in hers the minute he dipped his head and kissed her deeply, mimicking their joining with his long shaft hitting her womb.

When he freed her mouth, she screamed as her whole-body shook. Her hips moved in an uncontrollable frenzy when his shaft touched a spot inside her—one she hadn't known about. Within seconds, he shouted as he pounded into her, touching the mind-blowing area repeatedly.

Out of breath, covered in sweat, he continued to hug her. She felt him harden inside her. She widened her legs as far as she could; her nipples were hard points tingling in anticipation of his touch. He lifted himself with both arms. "We never talked about anatomy... We are true life-mates. Our bodies aren't ready to stop. They want my seed to be firmly planted in you."

"You mean we could actually sleep like this?"

"Yes, it has happened." His hips thrust inward.

"Ohhh. That feels so good. Do it again."

Still lifted slightly, he thrust inward again. She used her hands to push both breasts up and toward one another. She was about to twist her nipples when his mouth brushed her hand aside on one.

It was slow and tender this time. His mouth moved from breast to breast. He raised his head and smiled down at her as he thrust again. She stared at his mouth. It was different. He had fangs.

"Uh, Xander, did you forget to tell me something else? Maybe fangs?" *Why didn't he warn me? Is he going to drink my blood... Oh God, is he part vampire?*

"I think would be a good time to tell me what they are for?"

"Ah, my heart, we didn't have time for a lot of explanations, did we? Yes, they are fangs. Not all Xian's have them. I will bite you but not drink from you... I will give you part of my DNA, and you will give part of yours. This will make us one."

"Will it hurt? And should I do the same to you?"

"It shouldn't hurt at all. And, my love, you can do anything you want to. It will bring me great pleasure."

She smiled at him. He had done so much for her; she wanted to do the same for him.

She was so lost in the idea of biting him, bringing him pleasure, she was unaware he had shifted his hand to her waist and brought her up with him as he scooted back to the edge of the bed, with them still joined.

"I want to turn you onto your face and make love to you in that position. Are you all right with that?"

The pressure of his hands on her buttocks was driving her crazy, his fingertips sensually tracing along the seam. She could only feel and nod. She was putty in his hands.

He got to the end of the bed, lifted her legs wide and slowly turned her, maneuvering her legs until her rump was up in the air, knees beneath her and her face was in the sheets with her hands gripping the covers. Once in that position, one of his hands went around and touched her nubbin while the other went to one of her breasts, hanging free ready for his touch.

He moved his hips with slow thrusts; she moaned, trying to make him move faster.

He had bent over her and pulled her back to his chest; her legs were curled backwards around his, causing her center to be more exposed. He was licking and sucking on her neck as both his hands plucked and massaged her breasts. A breeze created by fervent movements touched her exposed nub. She had been panting, trying to catch her breath. When another small gust touched her, she screamed.

Everything happened at once. He changed the position they were in; she was face down. His hand was between her legs, and her hair was brushed aside as he nuzzled her neck and shoulder. He was pounding into her so hard the bed was shaking. He went still as warmth flooded her womb, and she clamped down on him, milking him for more. Fangs scraped against her neck, then his tongue. She pushed back against him, wanting one more thrust from him when his fangs sank into her neck. He was right, there was no pain. Instead, there was another surge of lust. She pushed back as he thrust forward, and his fingers plucking at her center, letting her nipples brush against the sheets. Decadence.

Lifting his head, he licked her neck. "We are one."

She felt him get smaller and slide out of her. He climbed back on the bed and snuggled me close.

"Will I feel strange with your DNA in me?"

"No, at least I don't think so. To my knowledge there are no records of how a female's body reacts."

"I hate to say this, but I'm hungry and I have to go to the bathroom."

His laughter filled the room. "Iona, go to the cleansing room while I order food. Then I'll go. When I come back, we will finish our discussion on the changes to our DNA... and how it can affect each of us."

Life Changes

Xander wanted to chuckle as Iona's eyes grew big and her jaw dropped.

"You're saying you change into a dragon... a real dragon and now I could too?"

"Exactly, with my DNA mixing with yours, there is more than ninety percent chance you'll be able to transform, like me. And so will Hester."

The very idea of her being able to transform... and where they could fly together sped his heart rate up. He pictured how beautiful she would be. What color would her dragon be? His dragon roared within him at his thought.

Iona's head swiveled to Hessie asleep in the crib across their bedroom. "This young? Really?"

"Yes, it is rare to see it happen under a year old, but Hessie has exhibited other gifts already."

"She has, what?"

"Have you felt anxious about something, then a calmness settles on you?"

"Yes, several times. Why?"

"That calmness came from Hessie."

"Did that come from your family or from the meteor on earth?"

"That I don't know. I was waiting till we had this discussion to suggest that Ranin investigate it. I felt you had the right to say, 'no.'"

"Thank you, and if it is Ranin, yes is my answer. But not Alain."

"Got it."

Iona moved from sitting beside him at the end of the bed to his lap with her legs wrapped around his hips. She rubbed her bare breasts across his chest. "So, when will I turn into the dragon? And when can I see yours?"

The thought of her becoming a dragon had him hard in seconds and his dragon urging him to bite her again. He wanted his mate, too.

Xander nibbled on her neck, using his hands he lifted her up so he could suckle her breasts. He paused. "I don't know when you'll be able to change, we can ask Ranin. All I know is I will show you my other self as soon as I can make sure we did the biting the right way."

"I want to be there when you talk to Ranin. I can't think of any but this," she rotated her hips, teasing his engorged shaft. "I'm sure I will have questions later."

He sat her down on his hard cock and bit her neck at the same time. She instantly climaxed and bit him. He roared so loud; Hessie woke.

As she got up to go to Hessie, she winked at him, "I think we got it right."

Chapter 8

Four Dats Later
Xander's Office on the Starship Seeker

"Your Majesty, this is the only way. I've run every scenario through my analytical system. Nothing else has a chance of working." Andrew's voice was firm and full of conviction.

"My friend, this is the hardest thing I've ever done."

"Your Majesty, it was and is my plan. You know, I've weighed the costs. The needs of thousands of people versus that one clarifies what we must do."

Xander extended his arm. Andrew gripped it just below the elbow in a warrior greeting and farewell. Turning to leave, Xander gazed at him over his shoulder. "You are smart enough to evade the Croffers and return to us. Promise me you'll do everything you can to do so."

Bowing toward him, Andrew replied, "I'll do my best, sire."

Bridge of the Seeker

"Sire, there are ten fighters and a starship headed toward us."

"Whose are they? How far away are they?" Xander stood in front of the real time display screen.

"Um." The officer cleared his throat. "Sire, it's one of the newest starships in the Croffers' fleet. They're traveling at warp nine -point-nine and have been tracked at over warp eleven."

"Not enough time to create a different worm hole or go through the current one and close it. Send alerts to any of our vessels or allies in the area for help. Red Alert, everyone armed and to their station." Xander turned his back to the screen. "Number One, send extra guards to the cover Healer Ranin and the Queen. Pull all the information on this starship. I want a briefing with the senior officers in my ready room in fifteen minutes."

He strode past the officers and warriors in their positions as all the alarms went off and the lighting switched to red. To the right of the command chair was his office door. It opened on his approach. His voice communicator pinged twice on his lapel. Tapping it, two holograms, one of Hester, the other Ranin, stood in front of him. "As you can hear, we are on high alert. Ten Croffer fighters and one of their new starships are set on an intercept pattern. They are too close to do anything but fight. Ranin, take Iona and Hessie to the safe room along with her two playmates. There are supplies already there for all of you. If you hear voices telling you to open, the code word is Manier."

"Sire, are we to follow the old protocol?" Ranin waited, holding his breath.

Iona had sat down on a chair near her and was swinging her head from one to the other. "These are the monsters that killed your brother. Xander, Hessie and I cannot be in the same location. They will abuse and use us against you. Place Hessie some place safe, and me, leave me in our rooms."

"Your majesties…"

"Ranin, follow protocol 202567. Not the old one. And do not let anyone stop you. I will not die, nor will we lose this battle." He raised his hand to end the communication.

"Mate. I will come for you and our daughter."

Touching his vcom, his last sight was of Iona crying with her hands held out to him and Ranin hustling to the door faster than he had ever seen him move.

He had gambled. If the Croffers took the "bait'—Andrew—that would give them enough time to reach their allies. If not, they were out-manned and out-gunned. It would end in hand-to-hand combat and with most of his crew civilians, it would be a fatal move.

He stood inside his door, "God Selenia and Goddess Oline, save us."

Xander lifted his head, straightened his shoulders, tugged at his sleeves as he walked into his ready room. Everyone stood as he entered. His number one paused, passing out data pads till he received a nod from Xander. Then he finished setting out the last few.

"Status."

"We are maintaining half a day's distance. Something is off, sire. It isn't like them to follow their target. Their fighter craft are faster than the *Freedom*. And with the new starship, they have enough to take us on." He half turned toward the view screen tracking the enemy. "What are they playing at?"

Xander pulled out his chair. "I'm not sure, yet. Scan long range... as far as we can reach. Tell me what you find. Any anomalies. No matter how small. Got it?"

"Aye, sir."

"Radar, start increasing scans. Increase by two hours per change. Make them intermittent changes."

"Aye, Commander Vente."

"Your Highness, what about the Queen and Princess?"

"Taken care of, Buel."

His Number One's received a message from the bridge. "A small craft left our rear bay; the Forward Controller wasn't able to lock on it long enough to read their insignia before it disappeared."

"Thank you. Let Captain Benson know we are aware and to continue monitoring." Xander tilted his head at Buel as he leaned closer to him. "Let's hope it wasn't noticed by anyone around us. Make sure it gets erased from the data files or marked as a training error."

Xander acknowledged the luck he had in selecting his mission team. Each member was not only highly intelligent and resourceful but also adept at deploying both intellect and brawn to accomplish their tasks. They thrived on unpredictability, using surprise as a key strategy. When Xander instructed Benson to resume work and Buel to clean up, Buel's understanding gaze confirmed his personal responsibility for the protective action.

Every military recruit endured tactical training, plunged into perilous terrains laden with traps and dangerous creatures. Equipped with a compass, knife, blanket, fishhooks, and fishing line, they were left to survive alone for three days before extraction. Xander's crew had excelled, achieving the highest marks across varied landscapes and weather.

He turned to the rest of his officers. "You have all the information Buel could collect on the Croffers' new starship on those data pads. Take them with you and report to your stations."

"Number One you're with me." He exited the bridge. He saw Buel open his mouth to announce him and waved him to silence.

The Center Radar Tech called out, "Sir, they are closing the gap. They are an hour away."

"Communications, put me through to the entire ship."

"People of Freedom Starship. You are all warriors of the Starship Freedom as of this minute. Our enemy has come closer, possibly to engage us. I am eternally grateful to have met you. Whichever home we go to from this moment on, we will overcome any challenges. Whatever we must do to win, we will do it. Our planet and galaxy will not be touched by them. They will not be allowed a foothold."

"Sire, they've increased speed and are thirty minutes out."

"Are comms still open?"

"Aye, sir."

"Upgrade to Security, protocol 101001."

He fought his own desires to be mate and *bormah,* instead of having to stay here as admiral and king. Inside, his heart was beating in fear for Iona and Hester, his old friend Ranin, and the entire crew of this ship. They were in a classic no-win situation. He was outnumbered, outgunned, outflanked.

No matter which way he went they would lose. So, he gambled. Andrew, his android, would sacrifice his "life" for everyone. He would literally be an unsung hero. And that thought hurt him. Some would say he was only a machine. But not Andrew. He had added protocols to it, no one knew about. It was more AI than machine, almost a sentient being. Andrew himself had developed the plan, and he knew in advance what it would cost him.

"All hands. No one takes actions for any reason until I, King Xander, personally give the order."

Xander stood in front of his command chair and stared at the view screen. "Radar, how far are you seeing and how close are the Croffers?"

"Sir, five minutes, and they are still increasing speed, not slowing down. Uh, sirs. They just passed us."

"Ship downgrade to Alert. Number One, you have bridge."

Secure Quarters

"Ranin, thank God. I kept expecting you for what seems like an eternity. Where are we supposed to go? I've a got bag packed for Hessie and myself." She did a quick head to toe scan of the older man. "Where's your bag?"

"Forgive me your Highness. I had to put some things in a 'pot', so to speak, before I could come. And we are staying right here. All four of us. His Majesty would physically fail if you were further away from him at this stage of your relationship."

"But..."

"He told me that protocol number was to let me know we were in a no-win situation, and he was going to take a calculated gamble that has a less than 1% chance of working. Apparently, it was a better gamble than he thought it would be."

"Why did he tell you and not me?"

"I don't know for sure, Highness. But I would guess it is because he is following his *Bormah's* example. He never consulted his queen."

"I think we are going to have to talk about that when this is over." Her eyes were grave. "Where I am from when you are married you are a team, and you don't hide information from one another."

"Err. Yes, Majesty, the two of you need to discuss it... but not when we are about to go into battle."

Before she could answer, there was a hard knock on the door. "Manier. Let me in."

Ranin ran to the door and flung it open.

Xander stepped in, shutting the door behind him. Eye alight, Iona ran to him and clung to him like a spider monkey. "You're alright? Nothing hurt?" She murmured.

"I'm fine, I promise you."

He lifted her hands around his neck, and when she opened her mouth to ask another question, he kissed her passionately. *God, how he could kiss.* She couldn't help but go limp against him and kiss him back.

Hessie screamed and cried.

"Hessie. It's okay, Mommy and Daddy are here." She slipped from Xander's arms and rushed to the crib. As she picked her up and soothed her, Iona glanced back. Ranin and Xander's heads were together, and she could hear indistinguishable words.

Carrying Hessie over her shoulder, she sauntered over to where the two males stood. "What are you two planning now? I don't know if I can handle it if I don't know what you have planned. I did my best to not get hysterical because there hadn't been time to let me know what was going on. But now, we have time. I need to know what we are facing. If I don't know, I cannot protect myself or Hessie if the need arises. I am your mate and partner. Which means we walk side-by-side, not you in front, and me behind you, like I'm lesser than you."

"I'm sorry, Iona. You are right, you stand beside me. Every scenario we ran, established we didn't stand a chance. The only thing I could think of is if they found out about you and Hessie. What they would to you both. I would have lost it completely. I probably would have agreed to anything to get the two of you back. Instead, I sent a decoy ship, with cloaking capabilities, for them to chase. It will give us enough time to gather our allies and get home."

Xander reached to take Hessie from her. Her pain and disappointment that she hadn't been included in any decision made her want to be such a brat. But she knew it wasn't fair to either of them. The fear for them was written on his face. He needed to know she was physically okay. Put away any anger she had. She gently handed her to him. "As far as what we've been talking about ... I asked Ranin to monitor both of you as we go through the wormhole. I'm not sure how it will affect humans or human hybrids. We should enter it .....," There was a slight jerk of the deck, then nothing. "Now."

Iona regarded both males, "Would it be alright to go back to our quarters? Or should we stay here?"

"I'll accompany you back to our quarters, then unfortunately, I have to go back to the bridge and send out some subspace messages to our allies."

The walk to their quarters was quite interesting. With Xander carrying the baby, she had the diaper bag, and Ranin had a basket of toys. She realized she alone might have caused some looks from the males. However, it was Xander's gentleness with Hessie and Ranin, carrying the toys as if they were the greatest treasure, that caught their attention.

As she examined the males they passed, she saw such longing for a child in their eyes. If she hadn't been searching, she wouldn't have caught it. It was gone in a flash. At first, she thought she was seeing things, until it kept happening. She's got to ask why they would gaze with such hunger. Couldn't they have kids? Was there something their bodies lacked because of their profession?

Kitchen Supplies Storage Bay

"Minor Receive."

"I'm in. Suit working. Will report when mission complete."

"Chith Off."

Chapter 9

Chith—Kitchen Supplies Storage Bay

"Warrior Tyne. Get in here now." Chief Master Byner's bellow bounced off the wall and hurt her ears. She lived in quiet. Loud beings like this fool Xian disturbed her, but she had trained herself to never flinch at any sound.

Chith cringed. It had been nice and quiet, and that shout ruined it.

"Chief Master Byner, you needed me?" Warrior Tyne rocked on his feet, puffed out his chest.

"Gods, I don't need you. If you are going to survive around the other warriors, you had better straighten up." He pointed at six racks of meat, a pool of blood and water under them. "What are these doing here? Where are they supposed to be and why?"

"Chief, they are meat racks. They go into the cold room. Because they are meat and can go back... I was going to move them today. They're not thawed yet. And the part that is thawed will freeze again."

"You fool. You would poison us with our own meat. We don't need any Croffers killing us when we have idiots like you working in the kitchen." The Chief grabbed him by the ear and drug him into the kitchen. "You are going to oversee them thawing and freezing. You will clean up the bay floor so clean Admiral Xian could eat off it. Do you hear me?"

Chith had heard nothing so funny for years. Maybe she should tell Singe the best way to kill them was not with knives, guns, or weapons of large destruction but by poisoning their food while in space. A snicker almost escaped her. Xian couldn't eat most of the plants or animals on many of the planets in their galaxy. It was the reason they had settled on Xandavier thousands of years ago.

The door boomed shut behind the Chief and the warrior as they left.

Good, she was alone. She debated on whether she should mess with their food, but practicality won out. Singe would want the ship, and if they were all incapacitated, she couldn't run the ship herself.

It was a quick climb to the top of crates. She surveyed the ceilings, checking for vents large enough for her to crawl through. Finding one, she wasted no time getting up into it and putting the grate back in place. She crawled for what seemed like hours when she heard a female voice. What? A female on a Xian ship.

No way.

Following the sound whenever she came to a junction, Chith waited for the female to speak again. She reached a vent overlooking a large room. A female was sitting on a chair talking to someone she couldn't see. She wasn't much bigger than a child. She'd be small next to her, and tiny next to any male Xian or Croffer.

Ah. She spied another vent.

What on Crossi! Under the new vantage point was some kind of bed, with bars on the side. A blanket covered a lump or was crumpled in a ball. She couldn't tell.

It moved! A tiny head turned toward her.

A youngling? Whose was it?

Could it be the female?

Hmmm. Wonder who the *Bormah* was?

Continuing her surveillance of the room, an old male dressed as a Healer spoke softly. He was standing near the female. Unable to hear the conversation, she spied another smaller grate between the two. Without a whisper, or disturbance of the air, she changed positions.

Who is the healer for?

Bing. Bing. Knock. The healer took a step toward the door when it opened.

A quick indrawn breath was all the display of shock she allowed herself. Xander Xian. The King himself was on board.

It was like a play, peeking through the vents.

She could feel a grin stretching her lips. It was so unfamiliar; it didn't seem natural, either. *Singe will reward me greatly.* To have the King and Queen of Xandavier in their power... and their child. Just like before. They captured Xander's parents and brother. The parents had refused to answer any questions, and Singe, in frustration, had cut off their heads and sent a *dat* chip taunting Xander at the sight of their bodies.

By contrast, his brother, Manier, after days of being tortured had murmured the name "Dina" in his sleep. The next day, they used the information against him. That was his last day. The torturer had hit him one too many times in the head. He died that night.

The minuscule amount of information from him made it difficult to find a female named Dina. Months later, they located her. An accident was arranged for her and her unborn child. Their informant had verified information that both the Mohan and youngling had perished.

Now, looking at this child, could they have lied?

Is this Manier's youngling or Xander's? Does it matter?

Without a qualm, she'd do her job—kill the parents and that pathetic healer. And steal the child. It took an effort to not smirk. They thought they were so clever. Ha.

Drawn from her thoughts and amazed at the female's antics. She kissed him and patted him. Asking if he was unharmed. Then the king kissed the female.

Can't hear them. She leaned closer to the grate. Seconds later, the baby started screaming. Her hands flew over her ears as she observed the female rush to the child and pick it up, soothing it. Then the king took it in his arms.

What the…?

Males don't touch younglings. That's the female's job. Strange, she had never heard of even the males from Xandavier behaving like this.

The thought of stealing the youngling from them and the upheaval it would cause for the throne and nation. She would be the next Queen with a Consort Mate. If she were turned to the Croffer side, Singe could train her to hate her own people and use her as an assassin against them. She wanted to laugh out loud.

Their voices dropped. She wanted to yell at them, "Speak louder and clearer. Your words are hard to distinguish."

It would have been wasted breath. The next minute, they exited the rooms. Chith followed swiftly in silence. Keeping them in sight until they took a turn down a corridor with no vents. Not even the shaft put in for future needs. She hit a solid wall.

Backtracking, she took the closest route parallel to the last one. Every inch she crawled, raised the hair on the back of her neck. Something was wrong. Of course, they did not know she was on their ship, much less this close to the royal family. She hadn't earned the title of "Invisible One" without listening to her instincts.

She stopped. Sat down and meditated, sorting all the threads that brought her to where she was.

The only discord she could find was the infant's crying—screaming, really. But babies cried when they woke up. The one she was raised with in the orphanage sure did. *Well, shit.* They didn't scream. This had to be a trap. Somehow, they had discovered her presence.

She scissored her legs to stand up, but they weren't working. Chith rolled to her side and put out her hands to help push herself up. None of her body cooperated. Furious, her mind filled with profanity. Her mouth didn't work, so her lips couldn't spew out the words. Her ears were functioning.

"She's here. I can see her heartbeat on the scanner." A gruff, deep voice spoke.

A sudden shout from that voice hit her ears. "Not there, you idiot. You'll slice right through her. I'll draw a circle on the ceiling, and you cut one foot outside the circle. Got it?"

"Aye, sir," replied a much younger male.

"While he is doing that the rest of you, get the catch net ready. We don't want a broken spy to fix, now do we?" It was a fresh voice. It touched her. She longed to hear him speak again. It told her there was a place for her where she'd be accepted.

A chorus of male voices replied. "Yes, sir. No, broken spies, sir."

Had her shaking her head mentally at her foolish thoughts.

Sparks flew from the laser cutter used to cut through the ceiling. The sound of the warriors dropping their face shields to protect themselves was a soft snap in the background. The edge of the vent floor dipped down, the hands holding the edge of a net beneath her were visible. Chith slid like a rock down a ramp into the net as the metal of flooring dropped at an angle, catching before she hit the floor.

Captured, two to three feet off the floor, with debris covering her unresponsive body. Only her eyes took in everything. Everyone around her was wearing a filtration mask. They had used some type of neuro-gas to incapacitate her.

One of the officers drew her eye. He was handsome for a Xian. He would make two of her. Ah, his rank. He was at the top of his field from what she knew of their military.

A sensation hit her when their eyes collided.

Hmmm.

Most males were put off by her markings, horns, and what they thought was a hideous color of hair. Oh, they liked her well-toned body, but that was it.

Weird, he wasn't looking at her body; he was focused on her face, her eyes.

"All right, King Xander wants to have a chat with our guest, so gently, lads. Let's take her to her new accommodations." He gave her a slight bow. "Sorry, they probably won't be up to your standards, but we try our best."

A joke at such a time as this. Yet, it made her feel strange, safe. *Why in the Gods' names would I feel safe in the enemies' hands?*

The rocking motion from the way they carried her in the net, and the amount of gas on her clothing made her eyelids heavy, until it was impossible to keep them open.

Iona Meets an Assassin

Xander kept blocking Iona's view. She took two steps back and stood on a chair. "You have got to be kidding me. That child is an assassin. She doesn't look over fifteen years old." Iona shook her head. "Can you imagine having to live with killing a bunch of people starting at this age?"

"What you are looking at, my love, is a person of forty-six years of age. Croffers, like Xian age, slowly. She was immersed in this profession from the time she was ten years old. She is deadly, and I believe this one's name is Chith Hilan. Her nickname is 'Invisible One.' If it hadn't been for our stealth radar, we would have never known she was on board."

"Still, I don't think she chose this profession. Something inside me is screaming she is not what we think." She caught Xander eyeing her like she was totally naïve. "I am not naïve. I think she is good at what she does to be able to stay alive. And that it was thrust on her by circumstances. And she has been living a lie, herself without a clue." She went back to watch the prisoner.

"What are you going to do to her?"

"Right now, nothing. She can't talk even if she wants to. The gas we used on her paralyzes the body. We'll make her as comfortable as possible. I am going to have Ranin change her into a hospital gown. I want to make sure she has no weapons on her."

"You'll put up blankets or something so that no one can see her, right?"

"No, she has killed with a hairpin in the past. I am not taking any chances with my men. She will not be treated like a guest when she isn't. Her abilities and use of them will determine how she is being cared for. After all, we don't want her to say we treated her like something she is not."

"At least don't put it on any camera that any hacker could find. It doesn't matter what she has done or is planning to do, no female deserves that humiliation."

"Enough, quit standing around. Let's get this going before that stuff wears off."

Fifteen minutes later, Chith was propped up in a chair, facing Iona and Xander through the bars.

Chith meets the King and Queen

Chith was conscious when the guards sat two chairs outside her cell, then the King and Queen came and sat across from her.

"When you have fully recovered, Chith, we will talk."

She settled back to think about this female and the King along with everything that had transpired.

Were they hoping she would turn on Singe?

He was the closest thing she had to a father. He had taken her in when her entire family was wiped out by the Xian attack. No way could she do that.

Niggling in her mind was the memory of her trainer who had failed. They all had thought Singe would hurt no one who had fulfilled so many of his impossible requests. They were wrong.

He had his clothing stripped off him with a whip that had ten strands on it. At the end of leather length was a sharp hook to catch the fabric of his clothing or skin and rip it from his body. He had died as his heart got hooked and pulled through his ribs.

Her body shuddered involuntarily at the memory. It was hard not to throw up when she could drink the water. Understanding what was waiting for her at her failure was something she didn't want to dwell on.

Xander

Xander watched any movement of her facial muscles. Any movement that would tell them more about her through the monitor disguised as a picture hanging on the wall in her room. He twisted around to face Tartar Khanate and Saarn Tunan.

"Don't be misled by her beauty or supposed kindness. She is as deadly."

Tartar opened his mouth, shut it. "I can handle her. No one touches her but me."

Xander sharpened his gaze at his old friend. "Why? Wait, she can't be... is she your mate?"

Saarn was choking on a sip of water he had just taken. "Your mate?"

"Yes, when we captured the assassin, our eyes locked and there was an essence exchange, I'm unsure if she is aware of it or the significance, yet. I will stand in surety for her. She will kill no one."

"If you are right, be careful. Once an assassin, always one."

Chapter 10

Eight Days Later

"What should I expect when we reach Xandavier? Booing and hissing? Or eyes only for you?" Iona tried to steal his covers.

"You'll be 'oooo'd' and 'aaaah'd' by all the public. And the Lords' that are single are going to corner me to find out where they can find such a beautiful female as a mate." He smiled and rolled over, leaving her naked.

"Hah." he heard, then he felt the bed move as she got off it. He leaned up on one elbow to see what she was up to. He had learned she had a quirky sense of humor. She walked gracefully, head held high, one hand on her hip and the other doing something in front of her. He couldn't quite see. He sat up fully, with bedclothes scrunched around his hips.

Iona went to the computer and whispered her command. She swung around and took a stance with legs wide and hands on her hips in front of him. Music with a deep beat flooded their bedroom. Iona swayed her hips in a figure eight, holding her hands above her head, moving until her back was to him. Every move matched the hypnotic beat.

Her back to him, she placed one foot forward, then the other one parallel to it, but spaced wider than her shoulders. Lifting her hands, she ran them through her long hair, head circling, whipping her hair—around and around. She swung her hips in a circular motion and placed her feet wider each time. At her first movements, his body had hardened. He was so hard, a touch from her hand, and he'd explode.

Oh Gods, his mouth was watering. She was swinging her head over the floor, her hands were on her beautifully shaped butt cheeks, spreading them. He could see her dark rose bud. She grabbed her ankles and pulled her head between her knees. From the bottom, she spread her lips and cheeks. The juice from her core ran down her legs.

He was aware she was flexible, but this. He moved so fast, gripped her hips, drove into her tight pussy. Using one arm, he held her in place, her back to his chest, lifting her off the ground. The other hand was busy running over her clit hard, then soft, slow, then fast. The way she liked it.

He felt her dangling legs reach behind and encircle his thighs. He drifted toward the bed, pounding into her in time to the beat, his hand doing double time. Over her shoulder, he saw her hands moved up and played with her nipples. Plucking and twisting, then pinching. It was amazing watching them swell with need.

Glancing up, he was in the position he wanted. Leaning forward slowly, she put her hands out on the mattress. His fangs dropped, and his body partially changed into his dragon form. He had her warned this could happen... He roared. She looked over her shoulder at him and smiled. She had fangs! And her eye shape changed to almond. She blinked at him, then chuffed a puff of smoke.

His dragon completely broke loose. His tail grew and swept the furniture into a pile. Her backside pushed against him. Nothing mattered but this.

Collapsing on the bed, he lay on his side, with her snuggled close to him. He was too tired and satisfied to speak out loud.

"Why didn't you tell me?" Iona said.

"Because I was just getting used to her, and you both were talking to me at once. At first, I thought it was you speaking in your regular tone, and then it was a feminine voice. I didn't know what was going on. Until one time... I heard her voice, and I looked at myself in the mirror. She showed me herself. I know you told me I could be a dragon too, but I didn't think she would talk to me... or let me see herself."

"Because I wasn't sure. It doesn't always happen with unusual species. And you are the first human we know that has."

"Oh, I think if Dina felt anything for your brother—like I do about you—I believe she turned into one, too."

Letting his hand roam Iona's pliant body, he pictured them in another position.

"I heard that," Iona said. "We can't. Hessie should wake soon, and we have an event to be at. Remember the one where you are introducing me and Hessie?"

Iona and Hessie Introduced to the People

Hester was dressed and with guards in the nursery. Iona was patting Xander's chest, telling him she needed five minutes, when there was a loud banging on the door.

Why didn't they just ring? He strode over to it grabbed the handle, yanking it open, ready to let the guard know in no uncertain terms they should ring, not bang.

He shut his mouth when he opened the door. Both Tartar and Saarn stood in front of him with grins on their faces. They pushed aside the guard. They were up to something.

Grinning back at them, he waved them into the main living room. A glance around made him wish he hadn't, but it was too late now.

"I see your dragon made his appearance." Tartar's eyes were full of laughter.

"And big time, I'd say. I don't think I ever saw him destroy this much furniture. He must have had a good time," Saarn chimed with a wink.

"Um. Yes, he did." Then Xander gave them a devilish grin. "And so did hers."

"What? That is such great news, Xander. Congratulations." Saarn was the first to say, but Tartar was the first to pound his back.

"Any signs of little Hessie having a dragon?" Tartar raised his eyebrows.

Xander shook his head. "It usually happens during puberty. On rare occasions, it can happen as young as she is."

Xander's hand shot up as he caught sight of Hessie crawling on the floor through her bedroom doorway. He held his breath, biding his time. A minute later,

Iona appeared. She was a vision, her dark hair piled high with curls cascading down. Her gown, snug at the bodice and flowing into an "A" shape, featured a pleat beneath her breasts. There, a broach, designed by Xander and bearing his coat of arms, adorned the gown. Her neck was bare, proudly displaying the mark from his bite – a symbol she wished to present to all.

It shocked him when she told him. No other queen had shown it. All he could do was stand tall with pride. He had a queen who wanted the world to know on all levels they were one. As she walked toward him, he scrutinized her. Something was different about her. He couldn't put his finger on it.

Right behind her was Ranin with Hessie's playmate/guards. Xander moved forward with his arm out, and Ranin scooped Hessie up. He wanted to shout with joy when he saw how sweet Hessie looked. In every way, she appeared as the princess she was. Including how her facial features established her familial likeness.

He caught Iona gazing at her, blinking her eyes, doing her best to hold back her tears.

A bell rang, and a guard stepped into the room. "Your Highnesses, it is time."

Tartar led the way followed by four guards, then Xander and Iona with Ranin carrying Hessie, Saarn accompanied by four more warriors, were their rear-guard.

Saarn and Tartar had strategically placed guards throughout every hallway they went through. Five minutes later, they were at the entrance into the King's Court.

The doors opened; music started blaring. Iona squeezed Xander's arm, and he grinned down at her. Together they walked in step, establishing they were one in all ways. He wanted her by his side, not behind him.

People fifteen feet away could hear those near the stage whisper loud comments as the King and Queen walked to the steps.

"She's so tiny, even those four-inch heel."

"Look at that dress, Monah, can I have one?"

"No wonder he says she's his life-mate, who wouldn't want that in his bed."

"Ouch, why'd you hit me, Norda?"

They climbed the six steps to the podium, side by side. Xander waved at the crowds, letting them know they should sit down.

Guiding Iona in front of him, he picked up the microphone from the stand. "It is my greatest pleasure to introduce you to my mate, my true life-mate Iona Shelby, and our daughter Hester Xian."

Iona placed her hand near his bite mark, and Xander pulled his shirt open to reveal his mark.

The crowd went wild.

"Together, we will rule Xandavier."

One Hur Later

Hessie was with her guards, and Xander had told Iona he had a surprise for her. He wanted her to experience something with him and now that she was formally proclaimed his Queen, it was the perfect time for them to sneak off.

The hallways were empty of guards. When she'd asked about it, all he'd said was Tartar and Saarn had taken care of security.

She wanted to pinch herself... a Queen. She, Iona Shelby Xian was a Queen. Who knew? Oh no! Now she handled an entire world! She who was barely keeping it together for just her and Hessie. Thank goodness she had Xander and Ranin. She was going to need all the help she could get.

She was struggling to keep pace because of her clothing. "Xander, what is the surprise? Won't it keep if we slow down a little? Where are we going in such a rush?"

He was walking so fast, she had to run to keep up. He had his arm around her, so every time she faltered or stumbled, he lifted her up and placed her on her still moving feet.

"What the…" He scooped her up and started running. Goodness, he had been holding back this whole time. What was going on? He was running so fast, and unbelievably, not jostling her. She could have been flying. That word "flying" made her look down. They were hundreds of feet in the air. She wanted to cry.

She had everything from her dragon but wings.

"It's all right," Xander said. "They will come when it is time, my love. Don't fret your dragon, she is growing as fast as she can."

Her pink cheeks changed to flaming red. *How had he known we wanted to not only see his dragon, but we wanted to experience flight? This is so romantic!*

"My human, together we will grow strong. We need lots of strength to grow wings and fly. One way to build up is to draw from our mate. The deepening of our bond will add power and might. Nothing can withstand us."

Iona kissed Xander on the cheek and caressed his beautiful horns.

"Mate, five minutes, and we'll be on the ground."

"All right, but no longer."

She couldn't stop touching him. His dragon was so incredible.

Chapter 11

Dragons

Her teeth chattering in her head woke her up. She was afraid to open her eyes. She honestly didn't know if she had been dreaming or it was real. Using her hands and feet, she felt around for Xander and her blankets. Nothing. No wonder she was cold. Crap, she was going to have to open her eyes. *Bugger it.* She popped them open before she could tell herself not to.

Overwhelmed, she scooted back until the rocky wall halted her. This was no dream. She perched on tree branches and tall weeds, precariously close to a 500-foot drop. Heights typically didn't faze her, but waking on this high ledge, with no barriers to prevent a fall, was a different matter. The thought of tumbling onto the jagged rocks resembling teeth below sent her head spinning and stomach flipping. None of the ledges she could see were as deep as hers. Fear rooted her to the spot. The realization that the ledge was not as spacious as she'd thought hit her with force.

How in the world had their dragons fit on it!

Her back pressed to the wall as she searched the sky for him.

Where are you, Xander?

He is the only one who knew she was a wingless dragon, and he brought her here. Ooh, she would tear into him. They both had changed form, shredding their clothing when they made love. Then he had flown them up here with the scraps of their clothing. With his body heat,

She heard a roar. It was Xander. She'd know that roar. From anywhere, the deep bass notes vibrated through her to her dragon. Who answered him? Surveying the sky, she spotted him. Something was wrong. One wing was making a full sweep... what happened? How hurt was he?

Two minutes later he quit circling and did an approach to the cliff top. As soon as his feet touched the ground, his transformation began. That's how they could land here. She had been thinking of their landing would need a runway. He didn't. Two steps was all he needed before shifting.

So furious she wasn't cold any longer, she took one step backward, then set her hands on hips, her back straight as a lance. She glared up at his face. "You better tell me quick, or I don't know what I'll do. Why did you leave and where have you been? AND how did you get a hole in your side that is still seeping blood?"

"Ah, my love. I left to get some clothing, and I went to the nearest village, stole them off their drying line. I marked the house so I can repay them." He placed a bundle on the ground next to her feet. Then he cupped her shoulders. "I was so happy. It has been years since I have transformed into my dragon. I have missed it so much, I decided I needed to check some of the area from the sky. My parents or brother and I would do it occasionally. Some *famer* mistook me for *tredator,* I don't know the word in your language. It is like a bird, but not a bird. Has a huge wingspan, can swoop down and take a *horsa, ocow, or famer...* you call them horse, cow, or farmer. They only nest on the highest peaks. As I said, someone mistakenly shot me."

Taking his hand, she led him to a rock to sit on. "That sounds like a *pterodactyl,* an ancient bird before males walked the earth. Now, let me look at your wound before we dress. We need to make sure it isn't still in you, and then somehow clean it."

She kept glancing at his face to make sure she wasn't hurting him. His eyes were closed, the expressions that flitted across his face went from surprise to sexual hunger. Mentally, she shook her head. He got hurt providing clothing for her. No one had ever done anything like that for her before. She wanted to kiss his wounds to show how much she cared about him, but didn't want to start something that could make his wound worse. They were very active when intimate, and he could start bleeding.

The moment he opened his eyes, he picked her up and set her on his lap. "I'm fine. One of the good things about being a dragon is my body spits out poison, projectiles, and disinfects itself as it heals at an incredible rate."

Twisting to see his side, he showed her the hole was half the size, and the blood had stopped dripping. She said nothing, just shook her head.

"You will have the same, since you now have my DNA." He nuzzled her neck.

"I wonder if that is why Hessie has never been sick. No colic, colds, nothing."

"Yes, I would assume so. Your sister having mated my brother would have had his DNA just as you do."

"Xander," Iona touched his chest. "If Dina had Manier's DNA, why didn't her body heal itself?"

"We would have to ask Ranin. But everything in her might have gone to fight for her child to live, rather than to heal herself."

Discovery

They made love before she dressed. Xander flew her to a hidden spot in a mountain south of the castle by five miles. She had buried her head in his chest during their flight. All she had seen was forest and rock. No place safe for landing. There was a cave carefully covered so that anyone who knew of it could stay out of the elements all the way to the castle. Lockers filled with clothing of all types, shoes, even jewelry, all set out to meet the needs of whoever entered.

She was drawn to something huge; it was covered by a large tarp or some type. Whatever, it was at least twelve feet long, eight feet wide, and eight feet high. Iona moved to it; taking one corner of its cover, she lifted it, but the lighting was so bad she couldn't make out what it was. She heard Xander's footsteps coming towards her. When Xander's hand appeared before her, she was playing with a corner. With one hand, he yanked the cover off and dropped it behind him.

It was a four-wheeled vehicle. The more she looked at it she realized she'd seen something like it on Earth. When she was little, for entertainment, her father would pull out family pictures albums from before he was born and tell her who everyone was. There was a picture of a six-passenger all-terrain vehicle. This was just like it.

"What is this? Is it a car, something like what you drove us to the Match Maker's office on Earth?"

"Yes, similar, because this is meant for rough ground. It came with us when we left our original planet over nine thousand years ago." He grinned at her. "We've kept it running all these yars. We called it a trans-vehicle, or TV. It is self-powered and moves silently. It is the only one of its kind."

Iona dropped all interest in the TV when he remarked so casually that "his family came here." "Where are you from? I thought you came *from* here. It seems like the entire population does, anyway."

"Our entire solar system was destroyed twelve thousand years ago by a nearby neutron star companion. According to the scientists, we had three hundred years to get everyone off the planet. Our leaders didn't waste any time. Fortunately, we had developed space travel, but not for the size of vessels we would need. Working around the clock shifts, our ancestors were able to get ships made for ninety-five percent of the people."

"What happened to the other five percent?"

"The seniors volunteered to stay behind. While the rest of the population finished building our transportation, they made recordings and written documents of our history. Vids were created for each family and placed in a protective container. That way, if the ship was damaged, our history would not be lost."

"How horrible, yet honorable. The words and vids of those left behind kept the memories of them alive for the rest of your people." Her mind went back to when Dina had talked about post-meteor things. How frightened she'd been because the younger people had rioted over food and other essentials. And when they were told there was no more food by the leaders that were still alive but were old enough to be their great-grandparents. They had retaliated with a call for all those sixty-five and older to commit suicide so there would be food for the younger ones. She had said it had gone over like a lead balloon, whatever that was.

All that she remembered after that was how glad she was she would never have to make that kind of decision. Now she was in a position where that could happen. How horrible to decide on who lives and who dies.

"I agree. I loved listening to them share when I was a youngling. It took us three hundred years to find this planet. The atmosphere, water, edible fruit, etc. were great. There were some indigenous people at a very rudimentary level, and most of the animals were ferocious. Our total population had dropped to seventy-three percent by then.

"We slowly merged into their society. Our people taught the children and the adults reading, writing, and the arts. We helped them develop a governing system. Before you ask, let me say we taught the good and bad in all types of government. Not just the one we left. The people chose."

"When did your people realize they could join with the natives?"

"Before we landed."

"By what margin were your family elected as the leaders?"

"The only family that agreed to run for leadership was mine. None of the others wanted the responsibility." Xander gave a tremendous sigh. "It has taken this long, nine thousand years for someone to want our position." He rubbed his head. "And I'm not ready to give it up. I would have if Manier had been found alive."

Iona stepped between the rock and the face of the cliff, wrapped herself around his back. "Thank you for giving me the truth. I love you Xander. And I trust you."

She stood up straight and tickled his ribs. She felt a wave of shock flow through him and heard his thoughts. What *is this?* "It is called tickling," Iona said. "Most humans laugh when their ribs or feet are touched lightly. It can be fun or torture. I always stop when I'm asked to, I promise."

"You need to stop." He let out a bellow of laughter. "We need to get back to the castle. I'm supposed to lead a meeting in an hour."

"All right." Would he fly them back or drive them? "I'll fly us back. It is faster."

Slavery on Xandavier

Iona was concerned when they landed. She heard voices, and their tone didn't sound friendly or welcoming. Xander was able to read her thoughts. Hopefully, he'll know.

"Xander, those voices sound really upset. Can we land and creep up on them so we can hear? Something feels so wrong."

"I agree. I'll put us down near the entrance. You'll have to stay behind me. I need to know where you are. Always keep one hand on my back."

"All right. I will."

They crept up together; it was Lord Iska who presided over the city of Zanda, the capital of Xandavier. Iska had a Xian on both knees, at his feet, with his head touching the floor. Iona could feel fury flowing like hot lava from Xander. If she lifted her hand from his back, he would have taken off to beat the lord.

"Am I hearing correctly? Is he saying to that man he is nothing but his slave?"

"Yes, Iona. You did."

"But, but...."

"Please, my heart, slavery is outlawed here. Whether Xian or any other species. But now is not the time to deal with this. I need to find out how far it has gone within the Lords. There is a Lords' meeting in a month. By then, I will have everything I need to replace those males and females who condone this and honor those who don't."

"All right, I'll wait. Do I attend those meetings with you?"

"Of course. My Monah never did, but you walk beside me."

"Yes, it is already on the agenda."

"Would you have me placed on the list to get copies of everything?"

"I will. I promise."

"Xander, please be careful. This is going to make a lot of lords and males mad."

He hugged her. "I'll tell you everything when we get home, all right?"

The Royal Suite

Grateful that their guards didn't blink at the way they were dressed. Xander's clothing was too small, and Iona's hung on her as if she were hanger not a person. Xander use mind-speak. *"Shower first, then talk about what we discovered?"*

Absolutely. My dragon might love a branch and grass bed, but I need to get it off me and out of my hair.

Their passion took over as they washed each other, then fell into bed.

Iona

I

n the morning at breakfast, Iona eyed Xander, waiting for him to bring up what they had witnessed the day before.

"Xander, if you have time, I'd like to talk about yesterday and how you're going to address the issue."

Leaning back in his chair, pushing his plate to the side. "Yes, we kind of missed that conversation yesterday." He winked at her.

"I've been thinking about it. I woke up several times during the night. Our people were slaves thousands of years ago and vowed never to do that to anyone of any race. Yet, we saw the very thing we told ourselves we would do. And it was a leader of our people doing it to a Xian."

She reached out a hand, rubbed his arm. "At least we are aware of it now. And we will do something about it."

He put his hand over hers. "You are so right. First, we need to have a special team investigating this. Find out how many are involved, and how long it has been going on. Our seeing it is not proof enough for the courts, especially dealing with a high-ranking person like Lord Iska. I know Saarn and Tartar could head this up, but it would take too much of their time from the regular duties. If you want, we can have a meeting with them or I can talk with them about who would fit the position, then do a second background check that looks deeper and includes their whole family. Only those investigating this issue and the two of us will know."

"I don't know the full dynamics of this and Xandavier, I'm okay with you handling it and briefing me on the side."

"I will contact both of them this morning. But, I want you to meet whom ever we pick. And you'll need to see their background, too. And if you have any feelings or sense that something is not right with him, you can tell me in private. All right?"

"Yes, I like that. And thank you for believing in my intuition." Iona closed her eyes, then opened them, staring straight into his. "This is going to take a lot of time, isn't it?"

"Yes, I'm afraid so. Depending on how deeply it is hidden, it could take years."

"Then let's get started."

She admired him when he stood and stretched. She wanted to pull him into the bedroom, but this was more important.

"Have I told you I love you this morning?"

"Yes, once isn't enough though, wouldn't you agree?"

"Yes, I do. I'm telling you now, again. And I'll probably tell you when you get home, too."

Iona attempted to sound impervious and arrogant. They were laughing so hard; it was impossible. She finally sputtered, "Now, go do your king stuff and I'll learn more stuff about being a queen."

He picked her up and gave her loud smacking kiss. "You're king will do as you suggest."

He wore a huge grin as he went to do his 'king stuff.'"

Chapter 12

The Market Place

"Your High… Lady Iona, please wait for us before going into any booth. They have posted your pictures all over the Xandavier. If you are recognized and something happens, the King will kill us."

Queen Iona's laughter filled the air. Scanning the crowd in Tekram, the capital's bustling outdoor market, she spotted four of her guards blending into the throng of people. Ever since her union with Xander became known, he had significantly bolstered her guard, two of which were also assigned to Hessie. Leaving a napping Hessie behind, she had persuaded Xander to let her visit the market, escorted, of course. It was a special day, celebrating their discovery of the planet now known as Xandavier. Commemorating the past, everyone donned garments reminiscent of styles worn nine thousand yars ago.

Iona wore a full length white sheath, and soft yellow overdress with embroidered flowers and birds found on the planet. Her guards all wore tights with knee-length shorts over them, and vests instead of shirts. This left their sculpture chest and arms exposed. They also carried a blaster in a holster on one hip and a short sword in a sheath on the other.

Captain Noer, the captain of her guard, gazed at her with concern. He was on his com when she saw his brow furrow. He sucked in a breath. Then he twisted around as if he was trying to locate his warriors. When he faced her, she recognized the indecision on his face. "What is it, Captain?"

"A merchant's daughter is being taunted and attacked by some males."

No! This isn't happening here. No female is going to go through what I did on Earth.

"What are we waiting for? Let's go help her." She tilted to her head to see if she could hear more noise in one direction or another.

"Majesty, you stay here with Sgt. Catri, Lt. Scont, and Warriors Mirts and Muna. I'll take Kane with me and help her."

Iona's back went ramrod straight, and her hands were on her hips. "No, I won't. You don't know how many males will be there. We are all going. I will be there to comfort the merchant's daughter while you and your warriors take care of her attackers. And that's an order." She leaned close to him. "Understand?"

Frustration radiated from him. Now he likely understood how the King felt when she pushed on a topic and won. "All right. You must stay in the middle of us. We will move at a fast pace. Don't be offended if one of us holds your arms to keep you with us."

"No problem, Captain Noer. I would expect nothing less."

They arrived in time to hear one of the bystanders in the middle of the crowd watching and laughing shout out, "Juna, you're no lady, you are only fit to lie down, and support your masters."

Four large males were dressed in costume like her guards. Their heights varied from six-foot five to seven feet tall. The young female was close to five-foot eight, tiny compared to them. They formed a circle rounding around her. Pushing her from one to the other, like passing a ball in a game. One of them had ripped her sleeve, making her top droop down, exposing the top of her full breasts. Tears ran down her face as she called out for her father.

Horrified at what was happening, Iona grabbed Captain Noer's arm. "Leave two warriors to protect me and take the rest. This stops now. Get that male in the crowd, too."

Noer nodded to the warriors, then at a nearby vendor with a large tent. He waved his arm at Iona to go with them. With a warrior on each side, she moved into the tent, going directly to the merchant. "Do you have somewhere I can see what's going on with no one knowing I am there?"

"Yes, my Lady, follow me."

In a position her guard could watch her, she breathed a sigh of relief. She had gotten there in time to see the whole thing; her warriors had arrived a second after she had gotten into place. As awful as the situation was, she also wanted to laugh. Her two companions and the vendor were totally absorbed in what was unfolding.

Noer entered the cleared area where they were tossing the female around. With one hand, he grabbed the largest male by his shoulder and yanked him out of the circle with one hand. When Noer let go of him, the man went flying into the crowd, knocking several onlookers off their feet.

Following his example, each of her guards chose one of the males. As soon as they stood close enough to them, with one hand they threw them into the crowd, knocking down some hecklers. The freed female crumpled in a heap weeping, trying to cover herself. A female from another booth dashed out and put a blanket on her and ran away.

The thugs, standing in front of the crowd of males, were yelling to those that were harassing the young female, "Go get 'em. You ain't doin' anythin' wrong. You gots rights." "Don't let 'em treat ya theta way."

Iona listened to the instigators and watched Captain Noer shake his head. These fools had no idea who and what they were fighting as they charged her guard.

Two minutes later, the crowd was gone; the thugs were in restraints, and the heckler from the crowd was chained to them.

Iona ran out of the booth with her guards as the young female's father appeared. "What is going on? Why are you in the road? Why is your dress torn? And where'd that blanket come from?"

The young female opened her mouth when Iona took control, striding into her father's booth. "Sir, where were you? Your daughter was being attacked. Why didn't you come when she called for your protection?"

The father took a step toward her with his hands in fists, his cheeks red. "I was in the facilities at the other end of the market. And there were enormous crowds that held me back."

She raised an eyebrow.

He took a step back and relaxed his hands.

Captain Noer stepped forward. "My Lady, this is Master Icket, the young female's bormah."

She eyed him up and down. "Sir, your daughter, Juna, was being mistreated by those males in restraints. My guard rescued her." She glanced around for them and found Captain Noer and the rest of her guard were fanned out, standing beside and behind her. No wonder the man took a step back.

"I want to meet her." Her voice was impervious. "Take me to her."

She wanted to laugh as he eyed her then her guard like mouse eyeing a cobra snake. "Of course, this way. My lady, may I know your name?"

"Queen Iona."

At her words, each guard had a hand on one of his weapons. Her voice had carried. Now the people realized who she was, and there were only six of them. She heard him whisper into his com for reinforcements.

A gasp filled the market as those that were close enough to of heard stared open mouth and in shock at their Queen.

Master Icket slammed to a stop. He bowed so low his nose touched his knee. "Your Highness, forgive me if I have insulted you. Thank you for helping my daughter." Taking a deep breath, he calmed down. "Please come this way."

Whispers grew into normal voices exclaiming, she was prettier in person than on the vid screen, and so tiny. A few questioned if it really could be the Queen and took a step closer, when a guard moved between them and her.

Unfazed by the stir her announcement caused, Iona kept speaking. As Master Icket extended his arm towards her, Captain Noer stepped in. Iona understood his action—she was too vulnerable. Current tranquility didn't rule out future threats. Icket, Noer, Iona, and half her guard moved toward Icket's booth, where his daughter, Juna, lay curled in a corner. Upon their entry, the young female lifted her fearful gaze, which softened once she spotted her father. A warm exchange of looks unfolded between them.

Ah, so her father cares. He was telling the truth.

Silently, Iona bypassed the father, squatted beside Juna, and cradled her. As she whispered soothing words, Juna wept, recounting how she'd retreated to their booth after her father's departure. Overhearing the males outside discussing their opportunity for theft, she was suddenly yanked into the open, manhandled, and tossed about. Through her whispers, she questioned why those she had known all her life had brutalized her. She wondered if she was to blame.

Iona's back was to the doorway. Masculine voices were, "Get out of the way. Or you'll get hurt." She lifted her head to see what was happening, then stopped, keeping her attention on the young female. Captain Noer and his warriors would deal with it.

A warm hand touched her back, Xander. Only he could touch her like that. She whipped her head around with a huge smile of welcome. For the first time, he didn't smile back. *No, he didn't... odd.* Her eyes roved over his face and down his body... Oh my. He was furious and trying not to show it.

His voice was very controlled. "What have you there, my love?"

Oh, he was going to wait till they were alone to yell at her. Good, she'd be ready for him.

The Royal Suite

Everyone had left them in their rooms. Xander was pacing. She could feel the heat coming from him. What had she done that was so wrong? No woman, no matter what her profession deserved that treatment. Didn't he himself tell Arnie to guard her and keep her safe no matter what? She had sat down when they first entered. She was tired of waiting to be yelled at.

"Stop pacing Xander and tell me what I did wrong. Tell me how saving a young woman from harassing males—that could have led to gang-rape is wrong."

He stopped in front of her, picked her up by the waist, and put her on a low footstool so she was eye level with him. "Don't you understand? I could have lost you. Without you, I end too. I and my dragon would die if something happened to you."

"Me, I wasn't in any danger. Captain Noer told me what to do, had me totally secreted me away so I could observe. You should know me well enough by now that I would never do that to you or Hessie. I know what it like to have no one." Iona wrapped her arms around him, kissing him all over his face and ending at his lips, where he took control.

She felt him put his hands on her waist as if he was going to pick her up, and she broke off the kiss. "No, none of that. I am angry too. Furious now that you're not kissing me."

She stepped off the stool and took his hand, led him to two chairs close together but facing one another with a small table off the center between them.

"I thought you said things were good with the people. What I saw and had my guard intervene was not good. It was horrifying. To know the males were egging those thugs on. Why? From what I saw afterwards, they all knew her and her father. Why would they allow it?" Her hand shook, then her whole body. Iona wrapped her arms around her middle as all the warmth left her.

"Iona! What's wrong? You are shaking like a leaf and you're so cold to my touch." He picked her up and sat her on his lap, enveloping her in his arms, tucking her head under his chin.

"Watching what was happening to that young girl brought back terrible memories... Only Dina knew about it. One of the neighborhood bullies had attacked me. The self-defense training Dina had insisted I attend had helped me escape." She shook her head as if to stop the thoughts. "Is there no protection for the females?"

"I didn't know this was still happening. There was a law at one time that if a female was not accompanied by an adult male, she could be approached. However, it also said if she refused to speak to him, he was to leave. Over the years, the law got twisted and turned to what you saw. With no adult male present to protect her, even if she refused, they could continue to pester her." Xander stopped speaking abruptly.

Iona was weeping.

He hugged her closer. "Why the tears now, love? It is over."

"I'm not sure. As you were speaking, I could hear in my head women weeping. And a soft feminine voice saying it didn't end with pestering, it ended with her raped and or killed... and her protector killed. It wasn't one female though, it was hundreds, maybe thousands. It is such a heavy weight on me."

Xander shouted, "Guard! Get in here."

Sgt. Kane ran in with his blaster in hand.

"Sire, is there an intruder?"

"No, put that thing away. Get Ranin and get him now. The Queen needs him." Kane touched his com and sent the message top priority. Then went to the door to alert his partner. He stayed by the door on the inside.

"Help me Xander. I hurt." She felt his arms around her and his knees under her. She was being crushed. It was as if she were in an invisible box, and pressure from the females' voices she was hearing was squeezing the box. She was being crushed. "I, hurt. Hard to breathe."

The sound of a snapping bone filled the room. Iona screamed as an excruciating pain ripped through her arm. She tried to move it; it hurt too much. A glance told her why. It had a compound break between the elbow and the wrist.

Gathering her strength against the pain, she lifted it when the door burst open. She jerked and screamed. Tears ran down her face that went from red to white.

Healer Ranin ran in, carrying a satchel over his shoulder. His eyes locked on hers. He slowed to a standstill in front of the royal couple. "What have we here?" He lifted a hand and gently touched her shoulder with one hand and moved Xander's arm so he could get a better look at the break. The moment he touched her, she cried out.

"I'm so sorry, Highness, I'm trying not to hurt you. When did this happen, and how?"

"Xander, please tell him. I ca… can't. Hurt." Xander told him what he knew of in the market, and Sgt. Kane filled in some areas she had not witnessed. Then he told her how she sat him down and asked why this could happen. He went over the law and its history. Afterwards, he had told him she heard female voices and crying and that it had been worse than he had ever been informed. Iona had said it felt like a weight on her, and it was crushing her. Then the broken arm happened.

"I have only heard of this happening once before."

"When! How and why?" Xander's gaze fixed on Iona. "Tell me how you or I can fix this."

***

Goddess Oline and God Selenia

"She is so fragile. Why did you pick her over Queen Hester?" Goddess Oline was so focused on the vision in the bowl of water, she heard him whisper. Tipping her head up, she said, "What did you say, my heart?"

God Selenia cupped her face. "I said nothing. I shouted. But why her?"

"She cares. Really cares. About them, even without me touching her, she felt their pain. She will do what needs to be done, regardless of the consequences."

"Why won't you release her? You have put her through a lot." He peered into the water.

"I need to fix this in person, and I'm going to need your help. It will take a physical touch from both of us... and Xander needs to see you, too."

"Why did you go this far?"

"Because you need to reunite with Xander.

"When Xander turned his back on you when Manier left, not knowing how his brother had begged you to hide him from his family... and he so longed for his brother, you wept for them both. Now, you need to bring healing to each other."

Without a word, he clasped her hand. Together, they jumped into the pool of water.

Chapter 13

The Royal Suite

Xander could feel his fangs dropping and his dragon fighting to get out to help his mate as he glared at Ranin. "What you do you mean this is not an illness, that it will take at least a priest or priestess.... or Selenia and Oline, the Gods themselves?"

Ranin stood before him as Xander continued to hold Iona. "I have only heard of this once before, and it was in an antiquities book on strange medicinal cases that only the Gods could cure...."

A wind blew from above them, scattering papers on a desk in the room's corner. The curtains billowed out, Xander arched over Iona. Ranin and Sgt. Kane both moved to cover them. The wind disappeared as suddenly as it had appeared.

As the males stepped away and King Xander raised his head, everything faded behind the couple now standing in front of them. Both Ranin and Kane fell to their knees, bowing before them. Xander felt like he was breaking his back as he bent over Iona, who continued to groan in pain sitting in his lap. He recognized them instantly. It was the Goddess Oline and her mate God Selenia... the one who refused to answer his prayers about his brother. As he bowed, all the pain and fury pushed forward.

A firm hand clamped his right shoulder; a softer one pressed his chest over his heart. Through the Goddess's blinding radiance, he saw another hand landing on Iona's heart. A sun-bright, masculine hand seized Iona's shoulder. The incomprehensible words of the Goddess and God reverberated through his body, their voices and power growing with each echo.

Forced to close his eyes, he saw his brother's desperate plea to Selenia - a plea to escape the Crowned Prince's duty and parental scrutiny, his brother kneeling, face buried in the floor.

Xander could feel tears run down his cheeks, as the scene switched, and it was him begging Selenia in the same way to show him his brother, to show him how to find him. Then Selenia wept in Oline's arms over the two brothers.

He mentally knelt in prayer with his face to the floor. "God Selenia and Goddess Oline, forgive me. I should have known without your help there is no way Manier would have stayed hidden so long. Thank you for the gift of his daughter. We will raise her and our children in your ways."

Slowly, the light dimmed, Ranin and Sgt. Kane rose and collapsed in chairs. Xander sat with open eyes as the light returned fully to normal. He lifted his head upward, seeing nothing as he shook it. "Xander, why do you look up and shake your head? Were you looking for someone or thing?" His mate's melodious voice rose from his lap. His gaze snapped down to see his Queen smiling up at him.

"Yes, we're you by chance looking for us?" Oline smiled.

"No, he'd know we're right here waiting to chat." Selenia replied.

Xander glanced up from Iona's face to see the God and Goddess sitting on floating thrones behind the chairs that Sgt. Kane and Ranin were sitting in. Both males were frozen. Flicking his focus to the God and Goddess, he waited.

"Good." Iona was pushing him to sit up. He sat up with his arm around her.

"Your Queen is alert enough to hear this too." Xander glanced at the two catatonic males as Selenia continued. "They can't hear or see. They can sense our presence, and that's all they need now."

"I forgive you. There was no way you could have known what your brother had done. And I ask your forgiveness for giving him everything he asked. It cost you both dearly."

The Goddess reached over and squeezed his hand. "Thank you, from both of us, for your promise to raise Hester and your children in our ways. They will always be in our sight. We will send several faithful ones to teach and train them. They are called Gods-Parents.

"They will have certain powers they can pass on to your children and train them with it. You will recognize them when they tell a tale of the Healing Emerald that you have never heard of. You must write these tales down. The children must memorize them. Through them, the Healing Emerald will be restored, and Xandavier will become the healing place it was."

Selenia stood on a cloud that appeared under his feet. "Iona, the pressure, and voices you heard were from the females from all the years of this planet. Females who suffered abuse and worse. You are the only one that has heard them for centuries. The small amount of pain you felt was to create empathy between you and all females, no matter where they are from. You will have an ability to help heal their minds and emotions. You will also, with Xander, have a responsibility to fight for them to be who I meant them to be." He let them view into his heart when he set his sight on Oline. "Helpmates, not chattels. Together, you will pass this on to your progeny."

He held out a hand for Oline. She stood next to him. "We are one, equal to each other. Let your union be the same." His right hand and her left hand lifted and flipped over their heads. Glistening multicolored sparkles like snowflakes from on their heads, in the chair and on the surrounding floor. They were so caught up in the colors they didn't realize they were alone, Ranin and Sgt. Kane was gazing at the spectacle in awe.

Xander watched as Sgt. Kane's eyes followed the glistening sprinkles. None fell anywhere but on or near the couple. "Sire, who was here? I remember kneeling, bowing to the floor, then sitting in the chair watching ..." He waved his hands at the sprinkles.

"Yes, Majesties. What happened? That's all I remember, too." Xander wanted to laugh when Ranin really saw who was sitting next to him. His eyes got so big he thought they'd fall out of his head. "Highness... Queen Iona... yo..you're all right." He fell back in his chair.

Xander caught the gaze of both males. "This is very important. Neither of you can say what you have seen or heard here... or felt. Do you understand me?"

Ranin nodded emphatically. Sgt. Kane gave him a confused look. "You have been in the presence of the God Selenia and his mate, Goddess Oline. As Ranin said, only the Gods could heal the Queen, and they did. They have a purpose for her. They completely healed her arm because they chose her.

"That is the main thing you need to know.

"However, someone might try to harm her, Hessie, myself or our world by taking her if they knew. That is why I must have your oath. You will reveal nothing other than she was sick, and Ranin had the answer. Can I have your oath?"

Ranin stood. He held out his arm with his knife in his other hand and sliced his arm till blood flowed. Xander stood, took Ranin's knife, and cut himself. Kane rose to his feet, held out his arm, doing the same. The three held their arms together, till the blood mingled.

"Thank you, my brothers. By the blood oath, we are brothers. Should one be in need, the others will answer. Should one need secrets held, we will bury it with them."

Chapter 14

Castle Dungeon Prison Cells

"Tell me why I had to come all the way down to the cell to chat with you? What was wrong with your office, Tartar?" Xander gave him a half smile. He had a pretty good idea, but wanted it confirmed by the male himself.

Tartar Kranatte stiffened at the teasing, "Chith. You met her." He rubbed his head with his hand. "I don't know which I can trust, her or the guards not to kill each other."

Tartar placed both hands on his hips. "That's why I've temporarily moved my desk down here."

He invited his friend and king to follow him.

"I just bet that is the reason. I'll know the minute I see you and Chith together if you speak the truth or not, my friend."

Together they fell in step as they chatted on routine things needed in the cells until they made the turn to the right where the hallway ended in a "T" junction.

Xander glanced at their surroundings. "Wow, I'm surprised you put her in this wing. This one has the least amenities. No privacy. And with only male guards... Iona would have a fit with no privacy to change or do her 'dailies' as she calls it."

Tartar gave him a sheepish look. "I had no choice. I put her in the other wing at first. She used that privacy to make weapons of things we had had never thought of." He shook his head. "Think about it Sire, a weapon out of a toilet paper holder."

Xander wondered if the shock that rolled through him was as visible as it felt. *Gods, toilet paper? What else could she do to harm his people?*

"I can see by your face you are just as shocked at the guard whose throat she held it at." He waved his hands around.

They stopped walking, and Tartar put a hand on Xander's arm. "We don't know how she did it, but she made it possible to cut someone with it deeply, but as thin as a papercut. I'm still trying to wrap my mind around it."

"Can she hear us? We're in the hallway of her barred cell."

"No, I put a sound suppressor on. It turns anything we say into whispered gibberish."

"Well, Tartar, I don't blame you at all if you felt it was better to move her before she escaped. I am keen to have a little chat with her."

Tartar glanced at his watch. "They should just be picking up her meal now. At times, the food makes her mellow. That's why I wanted to wait."

"Excellent, my friend."

They continued, nothing that they were seeing surprised Xander. Same gray brick walls. Every ten *fete* was a door made of metal bars. He could see inside. There was a cot bed neatly made, a sink, and a vid projecting an image that was purposely blurred. There was no sound, just images. He was going to ask Tartar about it when a prisoner came into view, and he had headphones on.

Tartar motioned toward the warrior walking towards, "He's got her tray in his hands." He stopped to intercept him.

"Warrior Timons, did the prisoner eat anything?"

Warrior Timons lifted the lids and then covered them back up. "No sir. That's five days, sir."

Xander shook his head. "*Daim* it. Call Healer S'tryker, to see how we can get food in her. She is not dying. And com me when the Healer is on the way."

"Aye, Your Majesty." Warrior Timons rushed out.

Before they moved forward, Xander wanted to say, be aware he could abuse her if he was left alone with her, but he had no proof. Instead, he decided discretion was needed. "I hesitated because I wanted to give you a female's perspective of Healer S'tryker. When I introduced Iona and Hester to him, she told me he made her skin crawl, and Hester almost split everyone's eardrums with her screams when he came near. That's why Healer Ranin came out of retirement. He's the only Healer Hester or Iona will let near them."

"You think he'd really…?" He lifted his eyebrow.

"Maybe not that, but I think he might not use a painkiller if one is needed, or not be sympathetic that she is female. He might also touch her in areas she is uncomfortable with."

"I'll make sure there are females there during the exam, and I will be right outside so I can hear what's going on."

"Good. I will not have us stooping to their brutality. Fighting in a battle is one thing, torturing when it is not needed is another. What the Croffers did to my parents and brother will be atoned for, but not by someone who had no hand in it. The person or persons accountable will be found and dealt with in the same way my family was."

Twenty *fete* later, both males stared into an empty cell. Everything that was supposed to be there was, except Chith Hilan, their prisoner.

Tartar tapped his com three times as sirens blared overhead, and strident footsteps grew louder.

Xander tapped his com four times, and the sirens stopped, but flashing lights came on.

"Sorry, the sound was hurting my head. And I'd rather she not know, you are aware she has escaped. With the lights, hopefully, she'll think they are about something else."

"You're right. Her size gives her an advantage. Sire, my gut is telling me we need more protection for the Queen and Princess but won't follow through on it. I know the quality of warriors guarding them. With your permission, I would like to have a chat with the Queen if you will allow it."

"Of course, but why?"

"She is the only female aboard. I know how to think like a male, a military male, I don't know how to think like a female. She might have insight into the situation."

The Royal Suite

Iona was playing with Hessie in the living room when a metal bang, ping, crunch, and a "*daim it*" came from the bathroom. She pressed her com button twice, letting her guards know something was wrong in her quarters.

She quietly picked up Hessie's pacifier and her favorite stuffed *reab*, the closest thing she'd found to a teddy bear. Holding the little one close, she crept towards the door, away from the bathroom, hiding behind any large furniture like the settee and loveseat. She caught the creak of the suite's entrance door made and glanced over her shoulder. Sgt. Kane was coming in with this blaster in one hand. Behind him was Warrior Mirts, who motioned for her to go out into the hall.

She pointed her ear towards the bathroom and ran silently towards the door. Outside, she ran into Captain Noer, who pushed her and Hessie behind him. Four more of her guards surrounded her. One of the guards, when she moved further away from the door, whispered that King Xander was on the way.

The attention of her guards riveted on the commotion within the Royal Suite. Iona spun around to see two of her guards sprawled on the floor. She knelt, checking pulses, and exhaled in relief when she felt their hearts beating. Her eyes scrutinized the hallway. No one was in sight, and she heard nothing when her warriors had collapsed. The hallway was full of potential hiding places. Heavy, curtained alcoves could easily conceal a pair of warriors, and the numerous guest suites lining the hallway could hide a full-blown army.

What an idiot! The noise in the bathroom been a diversion.

The hair stood up on the back of her neck. Tilting her head to say something to one of her guards, she realized Captain Noer and the rest of her guard were in her quarters. They thought she was protected when she wasn't.

Everything in her screamed for her to hide. She half-turned toward her suite, but the door was shut, which meant it was locked. Glancing down at Hessie, she sighed with relief. She'd fallen asleep.

Iona knew she couldn't stay there. She took off to the right. If she remembered correctly, there was only one window with a seat this way. So long as Hessie slept, they'd be safe there. She thought of which dignitary rooms were down this way. One she knew was for visiting royalty, is bigger than the other suites.

First, order is to find a place for to hide... She took her shoes off, stuffed them in her pockets, her socks wouldn't make any noise. *If she got caught or killed and Hessie taken... The entire Croffers nation would be destroyed. I can't let her find us. Her people will* use us to destroy Xander and all his people. Please, if any God being is hearing my heart, help us.

She didn't make a sound as she ran looking for the window seat. She reached the first one; after closing the curtain, she went to the next one. Ten sets of curtains later, she found it. Once inside, she climbed up onto the seat and listened.

"My dragon, please wake up. We need your help."

"I here. Why you so scared? Where's mate?"

"Oh, thank the Gods. You've woken up! It doesn't matter where he is. We must deal with this. An assassin is hunting for me and Hessie. I need you to listen and let me know if you hear anything out of the ordinary. I couldn't hear her, but you can. We've got to hide until Xander gets here."

"We need go other place, not stay."

"Can you hear anything? All I can hear is my heartbeat."

"We go in room, lock her out. Stay safe till mate get here."

You're right. She put her feet on the floor, took two steps and she was closing the curtain when her dragon spoke.

Hurry, hear feet, so hard to hear.

Running down the hallway, only able to hear the rustle of the fabric of her dress and her beating heart, when a feminine voice—just like the assassin they had captured—whispered a word, "run."

"Let her think you stupid."

"You're right, we'll distract her, so we have time to set a trap."

She held the doorknob and eased it into the closed position, letting a loud click resounded in the suite and hallway.

"I heard that. Oh, my little *mosue*. You gave yourself away. Think of me as the great big *tikky* that's coming to get you. I won't hurt you, though. I want you and that baby as a gift for a proper king. My King. Singe Lin Minor."

"You can try, but you can't catch me. Who are you to imply Xander isn't a proper king? For generations, his family has served as the leaders of their world. How long has your so-called king held his position?" Iona heaved a sigh. "He is the first in that position of his family."

"That may be true. It is his leadership that has convinced Xander, the male you thought was your life-mate; to turn you over to him and he would get to keep the youngling for his own. How else could I have escaped your prison? Humm. I had to have help, didn't I?"

That assassin, Chith, can't be telling the truth. Iona put her hands over her ears.

"You doubt me female. You'll see he is using you to get what he wants."

"We both know your leader wants to torture me because he likes to make everyone hurt, and to make Xander suffer. He won't even treat me as well as we treated you. Tell me I'm lying, go on. Tell me."

"You probably won't be treated as nice, that's true. We don't have your resources. But Singe doesn't like to hurt others."

"I don't believe you really know him. Because you can't challenge him without the knowledge, he'd kill you for doing it."

"You're wrong. At least I'm not lying to you. I've always spoken truth. Your supposed 'life-mate' is and has been lying to you to get that youngling from you. You'll see. If he can rescue you from me. He won't say anything about loving you."

No, I don't believe it. He loves me, right?

Catching An Assassin

*N*o, she wasn't playing that game. She had to trust Xander not some assassin.

In silence, she went to the suite's door. Opened it. The enormous bed told her where she was. It was the suite for visiting royalty. She laid Hessie down, grabbing the pillows to as a barrier for her, then flew to the door.

The door moved silently into its closed position. Iona continued to hold the knob; afraid it would click when it seated itself. Her ear to the door she heard a door open some distance away. *There weren't any dignitaries visiting now.... It had to be Chith.* Gently, she turned the knob to its resting position. Let out a breath of relief at the silence.

Her dragon whispered. "You smart. You set trap for her now."

"No, we are smart. Together, you, my dragon, and I will capture her. You keep listening for her, while I check out what we can use to our advantage."

Standing with her back to the door, she took stock of the room. There were two more doors, both ajar, the bed, dressers, nightstands with lamps on them, a love seat, and an easy chair. The first open door turned out to be the bathroom, with full walk-in dressing rooms and closets, which had another entrance from the hall. The other opened to the living room. After she closed it, she ran back to the dressing room and grabbed its chair. Then she propped it under the door handle to lock the door to the dressing room.

"I hear her. She not far." Her dragon whispered.

A shiver went through her. How to secure the door? She hit her forehead with the heel of her hand. *Of course.* The bedside table lamps would be perfect. Taking the one closest to her, laying Hessie on the floor, she took out the knife Xander had given her; then cut the cord cover and stripped it, exposing the wires. Afterwards, she plugged the cord into the socket closest to the door, then wrapped the doorknob in the wires.

Moving swiftly, she picked Hessie up and listened for the main door to be opened. She felt a draft under the door, signaling someone had entered the main room. Her hope was she would be distracted by the pillows scattered on the floor. So she'd check under the bed for them. When she heard the rustle of the covers, she slipped out into the hallway and took a chair, propping it under the doorknob.

The Royal Suite

"Captain Noer, where in the *helos* is my mate?" He and his dragon fought for control. *I can feel her fear. Somebody better have a good explanation. I'm going to kill someone if she is harmed.*

"When she ran into the hallway, one of the males whispered you were on your way as I put her behind me. The rest of the guards put her in the middle." Captain Noer stood at attention in the King's living room.

Xander stared at Noer so long he saw sweat beads on his forehead. When he walked around him, he saw it had stained the back of his uniform jacket. Xander placed himself immediately behind him. He pitched his voice to be a combination of himself and his dragon's growl. "Who did you assign to be with her?"

Wanting to rip him apart, Xander felt a little appeased, that the captain jerked, and his men jumped in fright.

"Sire." Noer knelt, and all his warriors followed suit. "I didn't assign anyone warrior. If you allow us, we *will* find her. Then whatever punishment you deem appropriate for us, we accept."

"Stand. Who was in the circle surrounding her? Each of you, come stand in front of Captain Noer."

Xander strode to the desk they kept in the living room and pulled a large data screen and some styluses out of a drawer. Carrying them, he went to a stanza sitting against the wall on the right side of the room, near the males standing at attention.

"You, Lt. Scont, draw the hallway and where you and the males were in back and the Queen's position in red."

He produced a rough drawing of two Xs, denoting his and Sgt. Catri's positions. He added a box for the Royal Suite on the other side of them and placed Xs for the captain, Sgt. Kane and Warrior Mirts.

Behind him were two Xs for Warriors Lear and Mund. He added the red X for the Queen in the middle of the last two guards, Banex and Tecan.

"Sire, I am unsure where the last two warriors were, but this is where their position was, Sire."

"They were on the floor, knocked out. That left my Queen with no one to aid her or guard her against an assassin who has earned the name of "Silent One." That is where they were, Lt. Scout." At his word all the warriors' faces reflected horror that they had left their Queen and Princess defenseless.

"Mund, Lear, come forward." Xander waited as they lined up in front of him, shaking like leaves on a windy day. "At ease. How did the Queen act? Did she say anything? How did she look?"

Naing, the most senior, saluted him. "Sire, she was scared; and the Princess was in her arms with her *reab* clutched to her. She said nothing. Her face was toward the royal suite as she kept moving back. I tried to block her. It was like I wasn't even there. She kept moving backward from all of us. I told myself that the last two of us would make sure she was secure."

Gods, he had wasted five mins trying to find out which way she headed and had gotten nothing.

His dragons all but roared in his head. *I know where mates are. Mate, call for me. Afraid. We find.*

The only way we'll find them is with your help. You lead us.

"Captain Noer, you and your warriors follow me, silently."

"Lead on, we will go where you say."

Chapter 15

Capturing Chith

When they were fifty *fete* away, Xander signaled "stop," with his fist closed. They all grouped around him in a huddle. "I'll take Lear and Mund. I want an officer with each group. Team Alpha, my team, will go into the first room; Team Beta, that's you, Captain Noer, will take the forward guard positions, whereas Team Charlie, headed by Lt. Sconts, will be our rear guard. And Team Alpha will secure the room. We'll rotate those positions with each suite."

Xander had one hand on the doorknob; he held his other hand up in a fist. Everyone froze. The sound got louder; it was coming from one of the next set of rooms. Xander quickly opened the door and waved everyone in. He shut it after the last male and heard a feminine voice. Had to be Chith, cursing, as doors were opened and not closed gently, then the rustle of cloth. *Bet she's looking under the bed."*

His dragon whispered. Mates not here. They set trap.

Captain Noer whispered to him, "That has to be Chith." Nodding, he let the handle go. Its click echoed down the silent hallway.

He leaned close to Noer. "I'm betting she thinks we are the Queen. Have the males spread out in here and the bedroom next door. There are the only two entrances from the hallway."

Xander considered Captain Noer and his team. They moved like a well-oiled machine. No questions, instant obedience. Each of those assigned to the living room moved into a position fit for their skill sets.

He could hear footsteps. They had to be hers.

Nice to know her plans. Now to thwart them.

They were coming closer. He could hear them, the others couldn't. *Thank the God and Goddess, he was a dragon, too.* He'd been fighting two battles at once. One to keep his dragon in check and hear what he was hearing, the other, keeping his own fury under control. *He was so worried. His heart hurt every time he pictured Iona and Hester. How did she get away? Iona was tiny, and many times, he had to slow down for her.*

Hum, a good question for her when he had her back.

Iona slipped out of the room on silent feet toward Xander and her guard.

Chith is Found

He had left Tartar questioning his guards about how Chith had escaped. And having a team inspecting her cell. He wanted answers, and he wanted them yesterday. No one had ever escaped their prison. So, who helped her? How did she get into the Royal wing? Somebody helped her… he wanted the name yesterday.

If Chith got out of the castle and into the public the things she could do. Her bomb making skills were renowned. Most couldn't be disarmed and so many innocent people die would.

The footsteps were outside the door. He set his hand over the doorknob to feel when she gripped it. He was going to yank on the door when she did and make her fall into the room. His lips stretched in a vicious grin at that picture.

The knob moved slightly. He held his breath ready to grab and twist it. Whoever's hand it was, stopped and lifted. *Shite.*

He could hear her heartbeat, no there were two. Without thinking, he snatched open the door and pulled Iona with Hester, sucking on her pacifier, into the room. He hugged them so tightly Hester whimpered. Loosening his grip, he said, "Do you know where she is?"

Violently, Iona nodded. "Last room. We just came from the back door in that suite. She's fighting the chair. I stuck it under the knob of the door in the closet between the bedroom and bathroom."

He waved Mund over, "Tell the captain last suite, she in the closet part. Do a two-prong attack. I want Lear and Naing with Hester and the Queen." Within seconds, Iona had a warrior on each side of her.

Xander let them see the fury he was containing. "You don't leave her side for anything, you hear me?"

In unison, they put their hands to their hearts. "Your Majesty, our lives for hers. We will not fail."

Xander turned to the others. "Everyone else come with me."

They moved in silent synchrony, like a well-tuned machine. Captain Noer and half the team approached the last door, while the King led the rest through the closet's main entrance. Xander signaled the countdown with his fingers, and on the fifth count, a warrior flung the door open their rush inside. Xander's group discovered an unconscious Croffer. Chith lay supine, arms stretched wide, hands bearing blisters and burns. *How did she get those?*

Xander touched his com, Command Center Responded. "Sire?"

"The Queen, the princess, and the escapee are in custody. We need a healer for the prisoner; we're in the Dignitary Guest Wing, we've left the doors open."

Ten long *mins* later, Healer Alain S'tryker and his entourage of three medics arrived. Xander watched him like a hawk does a mouse. *Why have I never seen how he treats those that look up to him? His denigrating comments and his sense of superiority is disgusting. his will not work out, I need Ranin find a replacement. This bustard's attitude will affect anyone involved in the medical field if it doesn't happen soon. They'll start thinking they are more important than their patients and ignore what they tell them when they are sick. Trust will be broken between them.*

Healer S'tryker bowed, "Where are the Queen and the princess? I will make sure they are all right."

"It is not them that need you to attend, Healer." He pointed to the female Croffer now sitting on the floor. "She is your patient."

Alain's gaze went from Chith to Xander and back again. "Her? Any medic can treat her."

"You will. She is important. She had burns on her palms. Take care of her so I can talk with her."

"But, Sire, I am the Royal Healer. I don't treat someone of her ilk."

Who the helos did he think he was. Healers heal, no matter who it is. He might be a healer by trade, but not by heart... he doesn't deserve the title, the little bustard.

"You will *todat*. You will treat whomever I say you will. If I tell you to go to *Mantiffe*, where they live in mud huts, you will go. Do you understand me?" Xander glared at him, hands balled into fists resting on his hips.

"Yes. Yes, Sire." He watched as Alain waved at his followers to shoo the warriors out of his way to get to his assigned patient.

Xander saw a wild gleam in his eyes and his face was flushed. "Sire, I need to take her to medical. She needs a full exam to ensure she doesn't have any other injuries."

"Do you have any female medical staff?"

"Yes, Sire we have two, a medic and an admin. Why do you ask?" His words were stilted.

"I want a full recording. You will be outside the cubical, the two females will conduct the exam. You can tell them what to look for and they will relay what they discover. No male is to be inside that curtain. Understand, Healer?"

His face was bright red. Xander was grateful for Hester's rejection of him. He would have missed the subtle clues of a male who had another agenda in mind for a female when she was defenseless. And he hadn't been around enough females to know when a male's presence made them uncomfortable.

He waved Captain Noer to his side. "Take four males and escort Healer S'tryker, his medics, along with the prisoner, to Medical. Stay there with them." He leaned closed to him, "Com me if any male goes in the cubical. Then yank them out."

He faced S'tryker, "Captain Noer and a team are escorting you and the prisoner to Medical. They will keep guard around her cubical until Admiral Tartar Kranatte and I arrive." His eyes followed them as they left.

Two secs later, Iona had her arms clinging to him and Hester trying to do the same as she babbled. Everyone stopped as it became clear she was calling him Papa. The first intelligible words she had ever said. After all, *todat's* fear came joy. He could even feel his chest swelling from her calling him 'papa.' He'd never truly thought he would ever hear those words.

He signaled for Lt. Scont. "I'm taking my family to the Royal Suite. Send Warriors Lear and Gaing to my suite. I don't care if you have to pull two men off rest to fill in for them. I want my family protected." Lt. Scont commed the two warriors, who could be heard running out the door.

Xander

*C**alm replaced my fear had once I saw my mate, and that the youngling was calm. In turn, my own fear disappeared. Then why did fear and fury flood through me the moment Gaing opened the door to our suite? I am vibrating with it. I could tell Iona hadn't noticed. The guards sensed it; they were monitoring him. Why was this happening to me now?*

The tremors seemed to disappear as quickly as they had appeared. He nodded to the guards. "Please take Hester into her playroom and shut the door." When he finished speaking, all he saw was their backside headed toward the suite's hallway. Then the door shut.

Xander faced Iona in time to catch her as she ran at him with her arms wide open and a loving smile on her face. He returned her hug, then set her down on her feet. The happiness in her face was gone and replaced with confusion and fear. He was flummoxed when she took a step backward and wrapped her arms around her middle. Her eyes were so full of pain. Her pain cut through him. She didn't say a word until she swallowed, stared at him with empty eyes and a blank face. "I was wrong, and she was right. You don't want me."

How could I be such a fool. She said he wouldn't say he loved me if he had saved me. I made all the moves. Not him. What a foolish idiot I am. We're married. I have nowhere to go, and Hessie. I can't leave her. I have to tell him it's all fake and it is over.

He opened and shut his mouth, like a fish out of water. Before he could answer, she spoke again, ripping his heart out. "Obviously, what we had was fake. And you never really wanted me. I was something to play with. Hester is all you wanted. My human blood isn't good enough. What are you going to do if she turns out to be all human, not Xian at all? Are you going to kick her out after she grows to love you? Is that what you do? Get females of any age to love you, then kick them in the gut?"

She didn't wait for an answer. She ran so fast she was a blur to their room, slamming the door, bolting it and, if he was hearing correctly, she used the strategy of the chair under the knob. He hoped she didn't hook a lamp up to it like she did for the assassin.

How could she harbor such thoughts? *I'd sought her his whole life, professing his love when he found her. As a warrior, as a mate, he vowed his loyalty. Gods, the torment in his heart. Who was this "she" she referred to? Damn it! Chith had twisted their bond with her lies. I must uphold my truth, the reality I'd always lived. I recalled Hessie's scream when Chith spied on them - a protective barrier. I had to convince her. Losing her was not an option. She embodied his existence. He would show her every day that she was his utmost priority.*

His steps were sluggish. The pain in his heart made it so hard to think. He stared out the window overlooking the royal gardens. Then it hit him. They'd been together for only two months and so much had happened during that time. Once home, he'd been so tied up in his duties he kept putting it as more important than Iona and Hester... Had she forgotten the God Selenia and Goddess Oline? How had they blessed them together as a couple?

He looked at the edge of the garden where the gate was. *Where in helos is the guard?* Then he saw her wearing her favorite red cloak going out the gate, running down the street. *How did she get out there? Is she's running away?*

Why did the long stem plants around the gate wave as if a breeze had swept through—on such a windless day?

What could have caused her actions and words? She mentioned a "she," and the only female she had been exposed to has been Chith. Had he been neglecting her? Everything had been overwhelming for him—how much more so for her? He would pay closer attention to her, and she'd have to come to some of the meetings like he said he would.

Tapping his com, he told Tartar and Saarn to meet him in his suite.

The sound of people talking in the hallway had him sprinting to the door, and telling the guards to have maintenance bring him a step ladder taller than the doors. He went back to stare at the door to his bedroom.

Chapter 16

Iona Kidnapped

He started pacing. Something wasn't right. His dragon kept nagging him. *My mate call help. We go now?*

No, I must make sure she isn't in our room. Then we go. I want Saarn and Tartar involved in this.

He needed to scream. He couldn't think of anything else. The desire to vocalize his frustration was scratching at his insides. *Wait, something is different.*

It wasn't his dragon. The bond he and Iona had also dealt in proximity. His body was rebelling at the separation. It wouldn't go away. She was the only cure.

He heard the guards talking to someone outside and then the door opening.

The maintenance person with the ladder had arrived. In walked a small male about five *fete* three *centar* tall trying to balance and carry a ladder at least eighteen *fete* long on one shoulder. Any corner he went around, the male would hit something with it. Sgt. Kane was chasing after him. Catching the knickknacks, he knocked some off the side tables.

Breathless, Kane came to a stop and saluted the King. "Sire, this is the maintenance male, Torano. I'll stay while he is here with the ladder, if you don't mind."

"No, it's fine." He waved Torano over to him as he stood in front of the door. "Put the ladder here. When I come through the door or call to you, you may take it away."

"Sure thing, Highness." He set it down, moved it one way an inch, fidgeting with it as he adjusted it in the opposite direction. After a few times of those antics, Xander grabbed it out of his hands and put it where he wanted it and climbed to the top.

He knew the maintenance man was laughing. This was not a laughing matter. "Sargeant, either you or Torano need to hold the bottom of the ladder. I'll get off it in a few seconds and don't let it drop or damage anything."

Both males gripped the ladder then raised their eyes to watch their king climb through the door-sky-light. Dust rose, causing him to cough. Iona was obviously not there. Where could she have gone? Had someone laid in wait for her here, maybe the person who helped Chith escape? Whatever had happened, they hadn't acted immediately.

The bed wasn't its usual neat appearance; instead, it was a mess, blankets bunched one way, a sheet ripped from the corners exposing the mattress... this was not Iona. She had fought whoever took her.

Something winked at him. A bright shiny object. It was her bracelet, her tracker.

Why was her closet door open? Jumping down was the only way out of the window. He jumped, landing in the center of the bed. Two seconds later the slats and frame broke from the impact.

Xander ran to the door, removed the chair and lamp, he motioned for Sgt. Kane to come in. Tilting his head toward Torano, he said, "You can take the ladder and go now. Send the other guard in on your way out."

Examining the bed, he could see where she had cried into the sheets, then tossed off onto the floor. Once Warrior Mund joined them, Xander commed Tartar and Saarn. Next, he contacted the command center reporting Iona's disappearance... and that he had seen someone leaving the royal garden at the back garden entrance, and the guard was missing.

Two *min* later Xander pulled Saarn aside.

"Where in *Helos* is Tartar?"

"He's undercover trying to find the leak. And doing his utmost to trick Chith."

"All right. I wish he'd informed me. I need his help."

Xander's cheeks turned a ruddy color. "Queen Iona has disappeared. We were involved in an intense discussion. She ran into our bedroom, put the chair under the doorknob so I couldn't get in, and then I saw her leave through the back garden gate. Or I thought it was her. Whoever took her was wearing her red cloak."

I was a fool. She had confronted me and locked herself away. That wasn't running away. I should have known she wouldn't leave the castle with Hester.

Saarn lifted an eyebrow. "What is this 'intense discussion.'"

Xander grimace. "I'll explain later."

"Understood, my King. To find them, we are going to need *doggos*. You know they can track anything, especially in the city. We can have a team here in five *mins*. They'll be able to sniff the bed and blankets. We'll find them."

Saarn waved at the mess his jump had made. "We need to verify that the assassin is in Medical, too. She may have gotten past Alain, which I think would be child's play for her. As to the damage I'm seeing here, the *doggos* will have some choice trace smells to work with."

Xander commed Noer in Medical. Angrily he told him the prisoner had escaped... again, then asked permission to lock up Royal Healer S'tryker. Next, he called the dispatch center to send two *doggos* with handlers.

Chith and Tartar

There had been no chance to tell Xander she had talked with Chith through the door before she fled without Chith knowing it. She thought she hadn't believed her, only to yell at Xander the lies she had spewed.

She had left the lamp wired to the doorknob and had used layers of cloth as insulation to open and shut the door, keeping it hot when Chith tried to open it. Letting her think she and Hessie were still in the room.

Chith had also told her about the history between the Croffers and Xian. How his people had hurt hers, almost wiping them all out. There were less than 250,000 alive. And though they could mate, fewer and fewer were getting pregnant. They were constantly on the run, no place to call home. And it all started with Xander's great grands and had grown to what it is *todat.*

Chith also went to great lengths to let her know that Xian's never joined with anyone outside their belief, ever. And if Xander said he loved her, he was lying. They had to keep their blood pure. She talked in a cadence. Iona had to shake her to stay awake. She realized by the time she had made it to their bedroom, Chith had twisted everything, and the way she spoke was hypnotic.

When he didn't hug her back, it confirmed what Chith had told her, making her cry because she thought he was going to throw her away. Now she cried because she ruined it herself by believing what she knew deep down was wrong.

That's when she pleaded with her dragon. *Can you call your mate?*

I can, yes. But you might not like the results of it. So, before I do, he is upset. He thinks we cannot love them. You believed lies.

She froze when a warrior burst into her bedroom through Xander's closet, and Chith was right behind him. *How did they get in? Is there a secret door in his closet?*

Before she could break out of her shock, Chith ran up to her and hit her on the chin.

Royal Bedroom

Chith snatched Iona's red cloak line with *minik* from the closet and put in it. Then she grabbed a black one as she helped the guard. She had made promises, wrapped the Queen in it. He picked her up in his arms as if she were a child and followed Chith out through the hidden door to the garden.

She raised her eyes to the sky and rolled them. It was the only release Chith allowed herself. Her frustration from working with this dimwitted male, who thought with what was in his pants. It didn't matter where they were from; males were all the same. Idiots. He irritated her with his sly looks and his attempts to touch her. She was ready to end his life. If he believed her promises, the universe didn't need any more like him living in it.

They approached the garden gate. As she stepped over the body of the guard who had been on duty, she kept her knees bent, lowering her height to that of the queen's. As soon as Vinit, her companion, was through the gate, she closed it. It was his turn to lead her where she could reach Singe Lin Minor. She had half the package he wanted; she hoped it was enough that he wouldn't kill. *Half was better than none, right?*

This was all unfamiliar territory for her, the first time she had been on this planet. She couldn't take anything for granted. Times like this, her situational training had saved her life, even if the way she had been taught was brutal. It had begun when she was a child. She still flinched when she thought of the beatings she had gotten when she missed any tiny thing.

She turned her hearing up, focusing slightly more on the surrounding noises. Vinit was making such a racket walking, his huffing and puffing, and the creaking of his gear.

It had been another set of lessons she had barely survived—Your enemy can find you by sight, sound, and smell quickly. And this fool failed all three. She even had to run up and readjust the cape on the cargo in his arms. The brush they had maneuvered through had torn the hood off her head. If anyone saw her face, they would instantly recognize her.

Strangling him was too nice. Chith felt her jaw fall open when the idiot shouted over his shoulder, "We're almost there." She had already counted four other people in the woods within shouting distance. Wasn't he even aware?

Stepping up her pace until she reached his side. "Why did you shout? Didn't you see the other four people in these woods? They will have heard you."

He lowered his eyes to hers. "I saw them. They'll leave us alone if they know what's good for them. People know to leave me alone when I come back from the Palace."

"Why?"

"I'm tired and have little patience. I'd as soon as kill them as look at them."

"Okaaay. Even for me, that would be over the top. Why don't you just hang a sign up on your place that says, 'Not a good day. Bother me at your own risk,' or something like that?"

He mumbled something she didn't catch. "Vivit, you need to speak up. I can't hear you."

He spoke a little louder. "Louder. I can't hear you."

In a near shout, he finally articulated. "I can't read or write."

"Was it because you stayed home and couldn't go to school?" Maybe he wasn't an idiot, just uneducated.

His face was toward the ground. "I cheated to get into the guard. I broke in and got the test the night before. I have a friend who had taken it before and passed with a high score. I memorized his markings and passed."

No wonder the big lug bought her scam of getting her. No one else had bought it.

Noticing he was getting nervous about telling her about those stories. "How much further Vinit? She has got to be getting heavy."

"Maybe four or five mins away by foot." He raised the bundle in his arms up slightly. "She doesn't weight more than my niece, and my niece is fourteen." He nodded his head at a tumbled down cottage with a thatched roof. The yard's weeds were up to her waist, and old furniture and equipment were scattered around the yard. It was going to be fun walking around all that stuff. "That's where we are going?"

She was right about the weeds. They brushed her waistline. And there were a lot of them.

Wonder what lives in them.

Vivit stepped aside at the door. "The key is in my vest pocket."

Who would want to steal anything here? It looks like a dump.

She pulled the key out, then opened the door. Her head cocked, she stared. Inside was nothing like outside. It was clean and neatly decorated. To her right, near a window, sat a *dat-bed* that looked more comfortable than any bed she's slept on, *sintel* covered chairs and sofa, top of the line food generator, plus an old fashion cooker.

Her eyes lit up when she saw the music player. She loved music. He had placed a giant vid-entertainer on the wall facing the *dat-bed*. It had to be at least eighty-five centars wide and no less than fifty centars high. She moved further into the room. When she glanced over her shoulder at Vivit, he was different. He had gone directly to a *dat-bed* under a heavily draped window and laid the queen down.

When he straightened up, he was taller than before. His green eyes shined with intelligence she hadn't seen before. He was watching her like a hawk. *Shite.* She missed something. He wasn't anything like the male he had portrayed in the cells.

Tartar's Love for Chith

Tartar's focus was on Chith. Why he had decided this was the best way to get close to her, he had to be crazy. Xander was going to kill him... and her. He'd felt the intense need to touch her, smell her, even after she had bathed—the underlying scent of her essence. Begged him to make her his. As soon as he had helped capture her, and they touched skin to skin, her face had already imprinted on his mind... she was his mate.

He had almost fallen over. What were the God Selenia and Goddess Oline thinking? She was his enemy, not to be trusted. Chith was an assassin of the highest order in her society and dreaded throughout the three galaxies.

He caught her scrutinizing him, and at her imperceptive nod of approval he relaxed. Abruptly, she put her back to him and sauntered over to the staircase. "So, what's up there?"

All his equipment and weapons, and the communications room were up there. "Bedrooms for my parents or brothers when they visit. They keep a wardrobe here, so they don't have to carry luggage."

Stopping at the foot of the stairs, Chith faced him. She waved her hand at the *dat-bed*. "Is that where you sleep?"

Chuckling, he shook his head. Pointing behind the stairs, "That's my bedroom there with a cleansing room." He let his gaze travel up and down her body. "If you want to use it, you're welcome to. I won't push for you to fulfill your promise.... yet.

Without a word, she went to his room and shut the door. He heard a scraping noise. He glided to the door and put his ear against it. Smiling at her lack of trust, she had propped his side-chair under the door handle.

Even outside, near the far wall, he could hear the shower. Pictures flashed through his mind of her stripping and lathering up that beautiful, lithe body, putting her hands where his should be. Tuning them into one. Reaching down, he rearranged his pants; he was so engorged there was little space in his uniform for him to put it, beside it hurt. *Blue balls. He was going to have blue balls from this brief encounter if he didn't handle it right..*

A soft muffled, "Oh, ow." came from the *dat-bed*.

In two bounds, he grabbed a chair, set it down next to the bed. Gently, he laid his hand on her shoulder, bent close to her head. "Majesty it is I, Tartar. We are in my home. Chith is here and thinks she and I kidnapped you. Do you understand?"

Nodding. Pushing the hood back from her head. "Head, jaw hurts. I understand."

"I'll get you something for it. Sit tight." He went to the kitchen and rummaged in a cupboard, then fixed her a glass of water.

Sitting up facing the room with the cape pooling around her hips, her gaze moved around the room to him. A visible jerk and swift intake of breath as he walked purposely toward her. He handed her the medicine and a glass of water. "I am undercover. Chith knows me as Vivit. A guard that turned his back on his King and you, for some time in her bed."

The sound of his bedroom door opening put an end to any further conversation.

"Hey, what are you doing over there? Don't touch her." Chith was beside him before he could open his mouth to explain. "She is not to be harmed. Singe wants her in pristine condition." Chith put her hand on his and attempted to pull it from the queen.

"You are misunderstanding. Let me go and I'll explain. I don't want her hurt, either."

Pushing her hand away slowly, he wished he could read her better. *Was she feeling the heat?* When she had rushed over, he was encompassed with the scent of his favorite wash, mixed with her personal scent. After touching him, there was another note in the fragrance. *She desired him. Did she feel how hard his entire body went when she was tugging on him?* He could feel beads of sweat trickle down his back. He needed an ice-cold shower if he was going to live through this seduction of Chith.

Holding her gaze, he said, "she woke and was in pain from the clip on the jaw you gave her. All I did was give her something for it I and some water to take it with."

"Sorry." She dropped her eyes. "You did the right thing."

Tartar opened his mouth to acknowledge her apology when the baying of *doggos* filled the room. He pulled his blaster from his holster and put it in the back of his pants. Chith didn't even try to take it. It was common knowledge the Xian had created a technology where they could tune a weapon, like a blaster, to the owner's DNA. She pulled the knife she had gotten off the garden guard he knocked out, then hid behind the door.

Slowly he moved to the nearest window, pushed a button and the curtains became a vid screen showing them the outside. It was King Xander with an army at his back. His elite warriors split on each side of him and two *doggo-warriors* holding tight to two massive beasts lunging at the building, baying, and barking.

Without a word to anyone, Tartar went out the door unarmed.

Chapter 17

Tartar

Once he was outside, he leaned against the closed door. He knew what he'd done would warrant the death penalty for them both. He prayed Xander would understand his need to be with his mate and free her from her past. As he walked forward, he kept his hands up. Only Saarn and Xander might recognize him, and he was betting his and Chith lives on it.

Tartar watched the *doggos* trainer give them a treat for a job well done, then escorted them to the back of King Xander's warriors.

Five *fete* from the door, Xander nodded to those at his side. They rushed him and carried him to the ground, showing him no mercy. He wasn't surprised they were harsh with him. They knew, from the *dog-*

gos the Queen was inside. What no one knew was she wasn't harmed, well, badly. Xander would not be happy. She had a bruise on her jaw.

Two warriors grabbed his upper arms with his hands tied behind his back and yanked him upright. That hurt. Getting his feet under his legs wasn't happening either. Instead of letting him stand, they drug him in front of Xander and Saarn. Then threw him to the ground at their feet.

Xander waved the warriors back, then squatted next to his head. Tartar rolled to the side, so he was facing him. Xander wasn't looking at him, he was staring at the house. His mate was in that house with an assassin.

He grunted, then shook his head at him.

He whispered. "What game are you playing Tartar, I could charge you with treason?"

"I'm getting close to Chith. She thinks I'm a dumb warrior who will help her steal the Queen for a romp in her bed." He closed his eyes tightly, then opened them widely. "Sire, I told you, she's my life-mate. Surely you can understand what I'm going through. I must find a way for her out of this suicide mission. Queen Iona is fine. I carried her all the way here. But somehow Chith has a way of getting off Xandavier, to where the Croffers are."

He leaned closer so ensuring only Tartar heard. His voice was gruff, half human and half dragon. "It is because I know she is your mate, and I know I can trust you. Saved both your lives. You really think she has a way off the planet?"

"I don't know. I believe her instructions are to make sure the Queen was unharmed. And that she was half of the 'package' she was to bring back. The other half was Princess Hester."

Xander into Tartar's eyes, praying he saw his sincerity, relieved when he nodded his head at him.

"Sire, we have got to know how she is going to do this. We both know torture won't work. All it will do is keep her mouth shut."

"All right, you'll go in a cell with her. And once this is done, you'll still pay for not clearing this first." As Xander stood, he whispered, "My friend I hope this hurts." Then he kicked him in the ribs.

He stood with his hands fisted on his hips as the wind blew his cape out behind him. He was wearing all his armaments. Fully aware he presented an imposing figure. Facing his males, "Saarn, take four warriors and take charge of this prisoner. When we bring out the Croffer, I want them thrown in the same cell. Elite forces with me. The rest of you surround the house. Only the Elite and I will go in."

As everyone moved into their positions, Xander scanned the faces of his Elite Warriors. "Do not hold back if the Croffer doesn't come willingly. She will gut you as soon as look at you. She is the top assassin in the three galaxies. Your job is to bring her out alive. I don't care what you do, but she is to be alive, you hear me?" Every head nodded.

Xander

He saw the shock on his guards' faces when he didn't have them break the door down or kick it in. He knocked. When there was no answer, he knocked again. On the fifth time, a feminine voice was heard, "Yes, who is it?"

"It's me, King Xander Xian, may I come in?" He could feel everyone's eyes on him. He knew he was acting out of character.

"Why sure, come on in and join the party." This time the voice was still feminine but stronger, no fear. He glanced at the warriors surrounding him, nodded, and held up his open hand. He lowered one finger at a time in a countdown. When the last digit went down, they burst through the door, with him leading the way. No one had their blaster out.

Everyone was using a blade. Some had pulled their sword, others a dagger, and some had a dagger in one hand and a throwing star in the other.

In a split second, he knew where everything and everyone was. He shouted, "Up." Then he ran to the *dat-bed* where Iona hid under a cloak. Sitting down next to her, he pulled the cloak away, "Are you all right? They didn't hurt you?"

Her hands were all over him, so he hugged her closer. "No one hurt me after she hit me and knocked me out."

"She hit you?"

"Yes, on the jaw. I froze when they appeared. I'm sorry. I'm so sorry I didn't talk to you."

The balcony to the second floor fell to the floor with a loud crash. The whole building shook. Xander pulled her on his lap to watch the melee taking place in the center of the room. A few warriors had fallen with the landing in the middle of the room, groaning. The rest surrounded Chith, holding a dagger. Her arms were so flexible and fast—she used the blade like a whip. She'd flick her wrist at his warriors when they attempted to get close her. Their blood splattered the floor and walls. Her reflexes were faster than his warriors. Time after time, she cut them with her knife.

"Why don't they just all rush her? She's playing with them."

"They are giving her the respect they would any top warrior, they will only fight one-on-one. Ten against one isn't fair or just."

"Do you have a knife?"

He let her lean back in his arms, so he could gaze at her face. "Yes, why?"

"I want to end this now." Pink crept up her neck onto her cheeks. "I've never shown you, but I'm very fast. Like in you can't see me move fast. It is something that happened to some of us on earth from the meteor. I can stop this if you will trust me."

"I'm fast too. I will give you my knife and be right here if you need me." Xander nuzzled her neck as he prayed. *Goddess help me, I love her so much, if she gets hurt because I let her do this…. Please help her.*

Wiggling, she almost fell off his lap before he stood with her in his arms. Then he set her on her feet and handed her his dagger. She pulled his arm till he was bending toward her.

"Thank you, you won't regret it." He blinked and she was no longer next to him, she had joined the warriors. They were blocking her. When she glanced at him, he called out, "Elite Guard, stand down."

All the warriors positioned themselves beside their King. All eyes were on Iona as she moved with grace toward Chith, stopping five *fete* from her. "I owe you for sneaking up on me and knocking me out before I knew you were there."

"Ha. If I hadn't been limited by my Leader, you would be dead now."

"What? What are you doing? Get off me." In less than two seconds, Iona had knocked Chith's weapon from her hands, pulled her belt from her pants, and used it to hogtie her. She sashayed over to Xander, gave him back his knife, with a smile.

Xander's mouth had dropped open when he saw how fast she was. When she walked toward him, he smiled. "You are incredible, mate. We need to really talk. Let's go home."

"Yes, we do, we can't have misunderstanding like this again. And afterwards we'll have make-up sex." She winked at him.

"What do you mean? Is it putting on your cosmetics? Tell me, what is this make-up sex? Is this something particular to earth?"

"You'll have to wait and see." She laughed. "This I promise... you'll love it."

"Then let's get going. I am very anxious to try this with you." He gave her a sexy leer.

Apology

Iona looked relieved when the door closed behind them. They had told Hester's guards to stay with her for a little while longer. She took Xander's hand in both of hers and urge him toward two chairs that faced each other. She left him at one, then went to the other, taking her seat.

Xander leaned forward. She quickly spoke up. "I need to apologize. All this is my fault." Tears rose in her eyes, and one slipped down her cheek. She used her sleeve to wipe it off her face. "Please let me say this... I was the one who listened to her lies. A female I had never known—I trusted her over the male I love and had never lied to me. How could I be so stupid? Can you forgive me?"

Xander stood; two steps later he lifted her from her chair. He sat down with her on his lap.

I couldn't look at him. I had wronged him so badly. And all his Elite Warriors knew it.

As the tears silently continued to drip off her face, she felt Xander nudge her face up, using his index finger. When she finally looked at him, he cupped her face with his hand. His eyes were full of love, and it was all directed at her.

"My heart, I love you. When you yelled at me, I realized she had planted some lies. From the experiences I've had, everyone is so vulnerable when they are in the position you were in. And added to that, I haven't been around a lot lately, I've neglected you and Hester. I haven't done what I said I would do... have you walk beside me as my partner. I owe you an apology, too. Can you forgive me and know that I want you by my side?"

Before he quit speaking, Iona was unbuttoning his shirt. When he stilled, she gave him a saucy smile. This was the beginning of makeup sex.

Xander

He felt immense relief after they talked things out and, like she said, he loved make-up sex. The things she did to him, some he'd never even heard of. And he was eternally grateful she *had*. She had confessed he was the only one she would ever consider doing them with. Then he'd really hit the pinnacle, when she told him it was because she loved *and* trusted him.

He was spooning her; he had one hand cupping a breast, with the arm under her side. The arm was draped over her hips with his hand holding her tummy.

His legs were curved under her. Her nipple pebbled in his hand and the top of his thighs were damp from her body juices. He plucked one breast then the other as his hand slipped down between her nether lips. His tongue was busy lathing her neck, then scraping it with his fangs that had dropped down the minute her felt nipples tighten.

Easing his hands down between her legs, he circled her bud and cupped her mound.

He flipped onto his back, raising his knees with his legs close together, forcing his swollen balls and staff in front of his legs. He glided his hands and picked her up, so her back was facing him, setting her on his thick rod. She was so wet she slipped all the way down in one move. He wrapped one arm around her and opened her full lower lips, exposing her bud to his balls. As she rode him, using his knees for balance, her bud and his balls rubbed against each other, creating friction in four moves. She climaxed so hard; it was his legs that held her upright.

She got her breath, and he moved again. This time pushing her forward between his legs. His nuts hitting her clit caused her to ignite, then when he used one hand to rub from the back to the front, catching her juices and massaging her entrance until he could easily add his finger to his cock. The other hand was busy dipping into her into wetness and using them to lubricate her brown rose. He loved watching her backside as she rode him. Using his damp thumb, he caressed and pushed at her back entrance until he could ease it in and swirl it around. She was so tight he was ready to burst. Lifting her gave Xander a view of his connection to her. He wanted it all.

Wrapping his arm around her waist, he held her back to his chest as he changed their position. This time her rump was at an angle with his cock buried in her. He leaned over her, lifting her slightly so he could touch her beautiful breasts and run his tongue and teeth over her neck. Slowly, he lowered her as their bodies danced. Their thrusts were so powerful, the entire bed was moving.

He returned to dipping in her juices, inserting his finger in her passage and rubbing her brown rose bud. When he felt her hand reach back and massage his balls, he couldn't stop himself. His finger dipped deep in her flower, and she screamed as she climaxed, followed by his own climax.

He laid back down on his side, where it had begun, spooning her. She looked over her shoulder at him.

"That was a first for me. I have allowed no one to touch me there."

"We can play like that until you can take me. If you want. Your backside will accommodate me just like your pussy did."

"We can try, but if I say stop, we stop."

"Always, my heart."

Iona

Iona sat up and yawned. Twisting at the waist, she was going to tell Xander to wake up. But he wasn't there. She wasn't in their bedroom either, for that matter. She was on a white beach, with snow-topped mountains in the background and crystal blue water on the other side.

Where was she, and how in the hell did she get here?

"I did. You needed to know something about the changes to your DNA that are good but can be used for bad. These are incredibly powerful gifts, and those that you love you'll do anything for. You might be manipulated to use them for evil to protect your loved ones. You must come to terms with being unable to use them that way. Because once you give in, you will do it repeatedly."

"What are you talking about Goddess? Xander explained everything to me." She stood and brushed the sand off her clothing.

"This is something he doesn't know because he is a male. It only happens to the females." Oline sighed.

"The way you are acting and sounding, should I be sitting down for this? You're scaring me."

"I don't mean to scare you, not knowing would be even scarier. Take my hand. We'll go to a comfortable and private location."

What can it be... Oline said not knowing is scarier. And that's supposed to comfort me? What if I can't handle it? What did I get caught up in?

One second, they were on a pristine beach, the next they were in a house on a hill overlooking that beach, and able to see for a hundred miles in any direction.

Chapter 18

Iona

The view was so beautiful, and she was so involved in it; she didn't notice when Oline had left her side. It took her a few minutes to locate her standing on the balcony with a great sadness enveloping her.

"Goddess, are you all right? You are so sad."

A huge wind poured down from above. Iona had to curl over to protect herself. The Goddess didn't move. Iona wondered if she was even aware of it. The wind died as quickly as it has risen. When she stood up, God Selenia had the Goddess in his arms, comforting her, and Xander was standing next to Iona.

From the arms of her mate, the Goddess asked them, "What do you know about me— becoming a Goddess? What do our people say?"

"What do you mean?" Iona glanced between the Goddess and Xander. "I just learned about you."

Xander wrapped his arm around Iona. "The Goddess was once a Xian. And Selenia saw her and fell in love with her. He made her a Goddess."

"That can happen?" Iona focused on Selenia.

It was Oline who answered. "Yes, he can. Unfortunately, some of the lower Gods were not so happy about it. The Goddess Natas attacked me. Before the transition was finished, she took me from my parents' home and killed my parents who tried to stop her.

It was my fault they died. But at the time I was so angry at Natas for what she had done, I put a curse on my people. I was two beings. Dragon and Xian. I cursed those females like me so they would die in childbirth if they married their life-mate.

After that, fewer and fewer dragons were born.

"Xander, you and Hester are the only ones left. I must apologize to you. Will you forgive me? I tried to bring healing by introducing Dina and Manier. But the Croffers found him. The real problem though is that Croffers are a race created by Selenia for balance of the universe. They were allies, life-mates, not enemies. Because of my curse, they became your enemies." Oline buried her face in Selenia's shoulder.

"That it explains everything." Xander knees went weak.

Selenia raised an eyebrow at him.

"Tartar, my general of all the military, told me the assassin Chith Hilan, is his life-mate. Right now, they are in a jail cell together. He is hoping she will recognize him as hers."

"Yes, that is why I brought Iona here, and Selenia brought you. Iona must forgive the abuse she received and somehow let Chith know she is safe here."

Selenia leaned toward her. "It is not in her to kill her mate. Her mind, body, and soul will reject it. But her leader will require her to bring him to him so he can kill him. And her leader, Singe Lin Minor is under the power of Natas. The only way we can break the curse is to set Singe free from Natas. And then your people can be united. He has been able to blind his people with the half-truths of Natas."

"What is the best way to do this?" Iona spoke up. *I can comfort her and help her deal with all the traumas she'd suffered. Maybe even show her she is more than what she has been told all she is capable of being. But what else can I do? I'm not qualified for anything else.*

"We are going to give you power to take care of it. You must be careful with the use of it. If you use it frivolously, you will lose it."

Seconds later, Iona and Xander found themselves in a bubble, with sprinkles falling over them.

Jail Cells in the Royal Palace

"What?!" Chith was beside herself and seething with emotions she didn't recognize. She wanted the stupid warrior with her, but there was something that didn't ring true. Something pushed the desire as far from her as possible.

"Don't care what you want, girlie. The king said he was to be housed with you, then so he will be." The jailer pushed both in and swung the door closed. "Ain't my business to ask the king why. It's my job to do what he tells me." He put his back to the couple in the cells and spit a wad of chewing *babaco*.

Chith made a face as his spital hit the ground. She had to jump over it or be hit by it. She stumbled, and a firm hand came out, lifting her by the shoulder back to her feet.

He walked over to the sleeping platform on the opposite side of the cell. "I'm tired. We both need some rest. Don't try, and fool yourself, you do too."

"I'm not sleeping on that with you. You can sleep on the floor." She stood with her arms crossed and toe tapping.

"I'm the bigger one, here. And unless you can beat me, we will share the warmth of that bed. Nothing else. I don't like audiences."

She wanted to hit him so badly. The audacity and arrogance. *He can't order me around.*

"If it's a fight you want, a fight you'll get."

She ran at him at top speed, planning on taking him down in one move. She jumped, quickly twisted herself around to his back, and wrapped her arms around his neck. If she did this correctly, he would pass out. If she didn't, he'd die.

She had gotten her arms around his neck when he slipped his fingers under her arms and broke them apart. He held on to them, lifting her up from his back and swinging her over his head. Her back slammed into his chest. Oomph.

"You weigh more than you look. Come on, let's get some sleep. We can figure out our escape later." Without letting her go, he carried her to the bed, pushed her to the back side next to the wall, then climbed on to the open side and pulled up the threadbare blanket over them both.

He could hear her muttering under the blanket. He smiled; it was a good way for her to let off steam.

God knows he needed that... He didn't know when he needed to really let off some steam this bad in years.

Nightmares

The slumbering female next to him thrashed around as she cried out. "No, please don't. I'll be good. I promise." Tartar slowly turned toward her and gently wrapped his arms around her, laying her head on his powerful shoulder.

"You can't do that! They are innocent. They did what you asked."

"Yes, I'll go stand with them. You are wrong, Singe."

Mumbled mutterings he couldn't understand came from her.

What had she witnessed that it hurt her mind so much she returned to it in dreams? Singe. Could that be Singe Lin Minor, the leader of the Croffers? How he wanted to erase that memory with his loving touch.

Wanting and doing were two different things. As much as he wanted, the doing might break her if it was without her consent.

Everything was going fine until she decided his body was her mattress. Her mound was pressed into his hardness, and her delicate breasts pebbled hard against his chest. She began rubbing herself like a sensuous cat against his body.

He untangled her hands and arms from his body and laid her next to him. "What the ... How come you are moving me? Are you trying to collect on that deal?"

"No, I'm trying not to collect with all eyes on us." His eyes flew to the cameras and back to her face.

"Oh." She could feel the heat rising to the top of head. Moving as fast as she could, she slid to her side of the bed.

"The only place that vid isn't pointed is in the corner where the bucket is. If you need it. I'll keep my back to you so you can have some privacy."

"Thanks, I do." She scrambled over him; glad she had pants on. Standing up made it much more urgent to get to that corner. Muttering about her stupid pants, she unfastened them and sighed when she sat down. As soon as she finished, the sanitary spray hit her, and a whoosh emptied the pot. Standing, she kept her back to him. She adjusted her clothing with a quick glance over her shoulder. His back was to her. "The facilities are yours. I'll trade places with you."

"Sure. I'll take you up on that." As he moved toward the corner, and they passed, she eyed him warily, but kept walking.

Taking his seat on the bucket, he peered at her curled up under the blanket with her back to him. "Chith, they can't hear in here. Only see." Her head moved the blankets in a nod. "Why do you look at me with such suspicion? Have I made you think I would go back on our arrangement?"

She rolled on her back; her voice was soft. "No one has ever been this nice to me before. Especially when I haven't been exactly nice to them. I don't trust easily."

"Is there anyone you do trust, your parents, a brother or sister?" His voice was as soft as hers.

"I have no family. They were all killed by your people. I was three."

"Your parents were in the military? And you siblings were old enough to join too?"

She flopped over on her stomach, glared at him and with a harsh whisper she said, "NO! Your people bombed us. My Dad was an engineer, and my mother was a historian. My siblings were twelve and ten. They were in school. I was at an enrichment center. It was an out of town."

He could hear her pain through the quiver in her voice. She had never really grieved. Whoever had raised her built on it and taught her to hate. "Chith, I'm so sorry. I can't imagine what that must have been like. I wish I could help you ease the pain. Do you remember where you were? And the date?"

Glaring at him, "Of course I do." She flopped back on her side away from him. "It was at Ungine on the planet Partorium, twenty yars ago."

The mutterings were clear enough for him to hear, *ash hole. Bustard..*

"I am truly sorry for your loss." He could feel her pain and he wanted to cry with her. "I've lost too. My parents and siblings. Killed by your people." She didn't reply. "I hate being in the military now that I know you. I hate the thought of being forced to kill you or one of your people. Even the regular warriors. I don't want to harm them. Only the ones who gave the orders. You." He saw her stiffen under the covers. "I don't blame you. If you were there or part of it, you were only following orders."

"My legs are going numb; I'm going to stand, so stayed turned."

As he forced his legs to stand, a chuckle came from the bed. "Wow, you have a sense of humor."

Smiling, he headed toward her. "I'm decent and headed to the warmth of that bed, so scoot over and make some room."

He was lifting the covers, sitting on the side of the paper-thin mattress, his whole being focused on the female in the bed. The clanking of metal against the bars broke through as the cell door opened. He caught Chith, tilting her head as he stood and faced whoever was coming.

It was Warrior Bodine, the guard. Tartar had received reports on his sleeping on duty, being unkept, and mistreating prisoners. Bodine pointed at him, "The King wants to see you now."

Tartar swiveled back to the bed and put a handout for Chith to go with him.

"No. My message was he only wants you. She stays. I'll take good care of her."

Never had he wished more for sound on the monitors. Until he went to Xander, he wouldn't know if he was lying or not. He knew Bodine had no clue who he was, too.

Two warriors were outside with cuffs for hands. He did his best to let her know he would return as soon as possible through his gaze. Bodine shut and locked the cell door as the other two warriors bound his hands behind him. Going up the stairs, he was sandwiched between the two. Every eleven or twelve steps, one of them would trip him and let him fall. He twisted two times, so he landed on his side. The next time, they made sure he fell on his face.

They escorted him with no other problems to the Royal Elite guards standing outside the King's suite. "The prisoner the King asked for."

One of them stepped forward and examined Tartar, then glared at the guard who spoke. "Where is the female? And he is hurt. The King had ordered neither were to be harmed."

The door opened to the suite and King Xander stood there. "What in *helos* is taking so long?" He couldn't see around his guard, pushed him to the side. "What! Who did this, and where is the female?"

Both warriors escorting him fell to their knees. "Sire, we were instructed only he required. And he fell coming up the steps."

Tartar caught Xander's gaze and slightly shook his head.

"Uncuff him, and you two." Xander glared at the escort, then dismissed them. He turned to one of his elite guards, "Get me a copy of the vids on the stairwell. Now."

He grabbed Tartar and ushered him inside his quarters, telling his guards to stay outside.

"Hurry, Xander, I need to see the cell we are in. That guard, Warrior Bovine, I am keeping track of violations so he can be fired and prosecuted. I'm afraid for Chith."

Xander called out, "Cell 22 on Camera."

In ten strides, they were watching Bovine attempting to molest Chith. He was wearing some bruises and bleeding. She was holding her own and then some. When Bovine pulled a pulser out, he leveled it at her, pulled the trigger, and she went down like a limp rag. She could think and see, but none of her muscles worked. The effects could last up to an hour or more depending on his setting."

Tartar's roar, potent enough to shatter glass, filled the room. Xander gripped him, swiftly alerting his elite warriors that Tartar was an undercover prisoner. He instructed them to let Tartar pass and to converge on Cell 22 to halt the ongoing incident. Tartar wrenched free and bolted, rushing to his mate who had suffered grievous harm at the hands of his people.

"NO!"

Chapter 19

Tartar Saves Chith

He had to get to her before anything more happened. No one was going to get away with doing anything like this to his mate, nor any other female. Pushing himself to run faster, pouring every ounce of energy into his legs. He faltered for a split second, when an excruciating pain ripped through his back. He ignored it. And kept moving. *What the helos was wrong with me? Pain ripping through my body, quit hindering, and instead empower me.* Still asking more from his body, he rotated one shoulder then the other; the sound of his shirt ripping filled his ears as he felt the cool air flowing over his body.

Gods, he was airborne.

What the frack.

Glancing around to see if a *terradory* had grabbed him. They were one and half times the size of a Xian male and could swoop down and grab one in its mighty claws to take back to the nest to teach their little ones how to eat.

Twisting his neck, he looked over his shoulder. The fabric of his shirt fluttered in the wind. Wings had emerged from his back.

Sweet Mother. What? The only person I know who had wings is the king. How did I get them? I had been praying for something to make me faster. And now I am.

As he made his way, he shoved everyone to the side. Nothing would stop him. He would make it in time. Half dragon and half Xian, he landed outside the cell. With the door wide open, he rushed in and yanked Bovine from between Chith's spread eagled legs. Her eyes were filled with terror... until she saw him. Then tears fell silently down the side of her temples. Thankfully, Bovine had only unfastened his pants and was pushing them down when he got there. He hadn't been able to rape her.

Oh, but he had continued to beat her after he used the pulsar. He remembered the vid he had seen with Xander. There hadn't been a scratch on her yet. There she lay half on the sleeping platform and half off. Her blouse was ripped open, exposing her to anyone who was monitoring the cell. There were scratches on her tender breasts and bruises already forming on her stomach and face. Her sides had marks that matched the toes of Bovine's shoe, which meant she had broken ribs.

Tartar took in all of it in one swift glance. He snatched Bovine up and held him by the collar of his shirt, slugged him one time before landing against the bars on the far side of the cell. He hit them so hard when he landed against the bars, they bent; by the time Bovine hit the floor, he was unconscious.

Where did I get this strength from?

Seconds later, the cell was filled with the guards, and his king who had followed him.

Tartar was holding Chith with his torn shirt and the blanket covering her. His wings created a cocoon for them. He didn't understand how he got them, nor how to make them go away.

All he knew was how grateful he was to have them. They helped him save her.

Holding her calmed him. His mind was scattered. One minute he was ready to rip any male apart. The only thing stopping him was he couldn't make himself let her go. Someone touched him. He jerked away and glared at Xander. It took a full *min* to recognize him. He wanted to spit fire at him. *Where did that idea come from?*

His ears were buzzing. Slowly, the noise dimmed, and he heard the familiar voice of his old friend.

"It's all right Tartar. You got to her in time. Now all you need to do is get her to Medical so she can be scanned and healed."

Tartar felt a tug on his arm to stand and tilted his head down. No one was going to separate them again.

"Tartar, no one will carry her but you. No one will touch her without your permission. We know she is yours and yours alone." He felt the hand lifting him as he cradled Chith in his arms. He nodded at his friend. "I understand. She needs help." Facing all the males in the cell and those crowding the hallway, he saw concern in their eyes as they lightly lit on Chith. Averting as soon as they could. The warriors parted like two pieces of wood when split, giving him plenty of room to leave the cell and traverse the stairs.

Xander was right behind him. His hand was on Tartar, emitting pulses of calmness, all the way to Medical.

Medical

Iona stood waiting inside the doors of Medical next to Ranin. Xander was never so glad to see her. He was going to have to explain to Tartar what happened to him. And why it happened. It was such a good thing that the Goddess had told them how it came to be hidden from them yet still in them. Until now, only the Royal family had the ability to change into dragons.

Iona would know how to help Chith with the assault and the knowledge she was now Tartar's life-mate and what that meant. The biggest fear was that she wouldn't accept Tartar. She would run and not be the healing bridge between their peoples. It could rend both groups to shreds. Yet, he knew this was the only answer for the healing to begin.

So many changes in such a paltry amount of time.

He had signaled his elite guard to follow him and the rest to go back to their duties. Xander kept physical contact with Tartar's shoulder as they walked to a cubicle. He was about to lift his hand from him when in walked Alain. Ranin was already standing at the controls for the bed. A medic had moved a regen machine next to it just in case it was needed.

"Here, here. I'm the Chief Medical Healer, and the Royal Healer here. I'll take charge of the patient. Retired Healer Ranin, you can leave. Your majesties, I'll ensure she is well cared for." Standing at the foot of the bed, he reached out to take Chith from Tartar.

When his hand was within inches of her body, Tartar growled, and Alain stepped back.

Xander couldn't believe what he was hearing and seeing. Alain was livid. No one was moving but himself. He abruptly faced Ranin and the Captain of the Royal Elite. Ordering them, "Get this, whatever it is, out of Medical. He is some deformed creature and shouldn't be touching the patient. If you must shoot him to get him to unhand her, then do it."

He almost laughed out loud when Tartar lifted his head. It had shifted halfway to a dragon's face, his voice guttural, "You imbecile. I am Admiral Tartar. If you don't get out of here, I will incinerate you where you stand. Do you understand me?"

Backing away, Alain waved his hands at him. "You don't have to be so nasty. I'm only trying to help. And how was I supposed to know it was you? You have wings for God's sake, and your face is malformed...."

Tartar chuffed some smoke at him. "Get the frack out of here now. Ranin is in charge, you blubber idiot."

Iona

*W*hat *I'm going to ask of this couple, they need to be treated right. Not put in a position of* *defense, but openness. If Xander hadn't kept close to me when I first got here, I would have been terrified. I won't let it happen to them.*

Iona pointed to warriors, "You two escort Healer Alain out. Keep him from coming back in."

Stepping lively, she went to Healer Ranin, put her hand on his arm. "This is your domain, no one else's. Do you what you need to."

She faced the two medics who were standing with their mouths open. "We need another bed in the cubical for Admiral Tartar to be next to his mate."

Behind her, things ran smoothly. Ranin checked the scans and determined the regen wasn't needed. The bed for the Admiral arrived while Xander was whispering to his now wingless friend. She was close enough to the three males to overhear some of their conversation. Ranin joined them as soon as he had finished with Chith.

"The power I had, and my skills increased. Is it the same for you?" Tartar's gaze bore into Xander's.

"Yes, and even more so when you learn more about your dragon. The two of you share a body and mind. Never forget that. And he can control you if you aren't careful... dragons do not count the consequences in a situation. They are all emotions. Oh, and if you meet your mate, if your dragon doesn't agree... I'm not sure what happens." He turned to Ranin, "What happens in a situation like that?"

"I don't think it matters. His dragon is so attached to his mate, just as yours is. Nothing will tear you apart."

A medic handed a hypo spray to Ranin, who stepped next to Tartar. "Admiral, I need to have you more relaxed. This hypo spray will accomplish it, if you will allow me to administer it." At his nod, he held the spray to his upper arm, and a soft *shhh* could be heard.

Xander assigned four guards to them, two inside their cubicle and two outside the entrance door to their area. Putting his hand out to Iona, Xander said, "Our work is done here for now. Let's go check on Hester."

Chith Wakes

*H**mmm so warm, don't want to move. Nuukkuu whooooooo. What was that? It was loud enough to wake the dead. Oh no. It was a snore.*

Chith tried to move her arms. Nothing. It wasn't like she was tied or chained, cracking open her eyes to slits. In one glance, she took it all in. It was a curtained-off room with two beds. The backs of two guards faced the opening of the curtain surrounding them.

She lay in a bed, conjoined with another to form a larger one. A male sprawled across it, dominating his side and part of hers, effectively restraining her with his arm over her chest and a leg over hers. She prayed it wasn't the detestable guard. As she trembled uncontrollably, she noted the man sharing her bed had a different hair color and lacked the guard's repulsive odor. Despite her fear, a calmness washed over her, soothing like beach waves, eventually lulling her into a dark, heavy sleep.

*S**ix Hurs Later*

What woke her up? Chith moved her legs and her upper body. It was cooler. She shivered.

She opened her eyes in time to see Vivit push the curtain aside, then swiftly closed it. He only had on his pants. Images of him flew through her mind. She thought of how he enfolded her while he sat on his lap. He had wings attached. Now, she screamed as it all flooded back—the fear when he was taken from their cell. Then the guard came back. The fighting.

She was winning. He was pretty torn up and she had no wounds... then he pulled a pulsar from his back pocket and shot her. It hurt so badly until her whole body went numb. For once, she was glad her body couldn't feel anything. He had hit her so hard and kicked her with those metal toed boots. Tossed her around like a rag doll. She could see it, hear it, couldn't defend herself or even scream.

Then he tore her blouse open. She was unable to feel how he raked his nails over her, pinched and bit her.... Then he had gone back to slapping her face and dragging her around by her hair. He'd placed her on the bed, and yanked off her pants and pulled her legs apart. She felt the tears slide down the side of her face and gather in her ears. No male had ever done that to her. Chith's eyes filled with horror. *I couldn't stop him.* She'd killed males who had done this to other females, never thinking it could happen to her.

She witnessed him opening his belt and pants, pushing them down. *If only I could move, I'd cut off that worthless appendage. I need to see this; I will avenge myself. He'll never do this to anyone else. Gods! Stop him. I've never asked for your help since my family died. Help me, please.*

He ran his hand over his extending cock and smiled at her. "This is going to hurt you and be so much fun for me." He leaned over her, positioning himself at her entrance, and all she saw were huge black wings and a hand twice the size of his ripped him off her. He picked her up with the care of *Monah* tending to her hurt infant, setting her on his lap. Afterwards he covered her with his shirt that was in shreds and the thin blanket, followed by huge wings that came around, cocooning them both. And the blackness descended.

The sound of a curtain moving over a curtain rod and soft voices woke her this time. Pretending she was asleep she muttered and turned her head, opening her eyes a slit. Instead of a peek at what was going on she got a slap across her butt. "Come on, sleepyhead. Time to get up. I can tell by your heart rate you are awake."

It was Vivit's voice, and he sounded happy. Slowly sitting up, she realized she could feel no pain. *What was this?* When she had been in fights before, it took forever to get over the pain... she let no one know if she was in pain. It would make her vulnerable.

He pushed her hair out of her face and stood right in front of her with a crazy grin, holding a tray of food and drinks for two.

"Are you always this chipper in the morning?" She eyed him, did a quick check to make sure she was covered. "What the ..." She glared at him. "Where did these clothes come from, and who dressed me? Was it you?"

He held up his hand palm facing her in a peaceful gesture. "I'll answer those in reverse. No, Queen Iona dressed you, and they are her clothes. No man was in the cubicle when while she was making you decent. And there are shoes on the floor beside your bed, too. She was worried you'd get cold." He pulled a small table from the end of the room and unloaded the tray on it. Then he handed her a napkin and a fork. "Dig in. I promise it is good."

She tilted her head at him. "Why is she being nice to me? I knocked her out and kidnapped her." Absent-mindedly she forked a piece of meat and put it in her mouth. As she chewed, she moaned beautifully. Seasoned tender *chike*, covered with a *mashrom satee*, flooded her tastebuds. Under her eyelashes, she noticed he stiffened when she moaned. Was it not customary to make noise when food was this good?

"I'm glad you are enjoying the food I picked for us. I hoped it would find favor with you."

They both finished all the food he had brought and drained the beverages. "Um, Vivit, where are the facilities?"

"Across the hall. I'll open the curtain fully and keep watch while you take care of yourself." With a nod, she ran across and opened the door.

Ahhhh. What a relief. Could he hear that? She quickly flushed the toilet.

When she came out, he'd shoved the beds to the side and two easy chairs faced one another with the table in the middle. All signs of the food and tray were gone. She stared at the setting and lifted her gaze to him.

"There are some things we need to talk about. You might get mad, and I didn't want you to throw dishes at me. Otherwise, I'm hoping I will make you happy."

With a careless nod, she took the chair with its back to the wall.

He sat down, leaned forward with his hands clasped between his knees. "My name is not Vivit. I was undercover, I am Admiral Tartar Kranatte, head of all military for Xandavier... and your mate." He sat back.

It didn't take a genius to realize he was expecting her to be furious at the subterfuge and the mate thing. "I suspected during our trek to the cabin, then once inside I knew. You weren't who you said you were. I've just played along. As for being your mate, what makes you so sure?"

"I knew the minute I saw a picture of you. You see, my people recognize our life-mates in the flesh or by pictures. When we were kidnapping the queen, I knew absolutely."

"I am your enemy. I must go back to my people."

"Tell me this, what do you have to go back there for? Are you saying you are mated?"

Her eyes widened as he seemed to get larger. "No, I'm not mated. I have friends and co-workers."

He ran his hand over his face. "As crazy as it may sound, I love you. And will do everything I can to make you happy.... I have one other thing you need to know before this goes any further. Remember, you told me Xian's' killed your family?"

"Yes. But I don't blame you for it."

He stood, went to his bed, pulled a data pad and papers from under the covers. "While you slept, I went digging. During the time you told me about, I couldn't remember sending any battleship to that planet. I printed out copies of the duty roster and deployments during those dates, plus three months before and after it. I also downloaded some vids I found from that colony from that day, showing the planes strafing the city." He handed them to her. "I'm going to step out and let you read them. I have only lied to you about who I am. Nothing else."

Chapter 20

Re-united

When Tartar came back to face Chith, what he saw stopped him in his tracks. Iona was holding Princess Hester and letting Chith play with her. And Xander was calm about it?

Chith was the first to notice him. She greeted him with a welcoming smile. *What is going on? She doesn't hate me. That's good.*

When she waved him over to her side, the others saw him.

Before he could sit down, Xander stood and wrapped him in an enormous hug, lifting him off the floor. Iona came and gave him a gentle one when his friend set him down. Saarn walked in during all the embracing and joined in. Chith started laughing a pointing a finger at him. Which started everyone chuckling.

As soon as he could, he sat next to her. He put his arm around her and wonders never ceased as she leaned into him. He didn't know whether to jump, or shout with joy.

Xander eyed him. "While you were out giving Chith some time alone, she asked the guard to contact us. She wanted us to join the two of you." He glanced at him, then at Chith and back to him. "She said you shared some information with her about our troop movements around twenty years ago. She also wanted us here as witnesses to her response to it."

Chith clasped his hand between the two of hers. "Thank you. You have given me something I'd never had before… honesty and freedom. I truly believe the ships that bombed the city we lived in were from my own people. They were killed because they had refused to fight your people. They didn't understand why a race we had been allies with for so long we were now supposed to fight. Those of us that survived were told over and over the Xian had done this. And that was why we had to go to war. While I read the reports and watched the vids, I had flashbacks of before, during and after the bombing." She blinked back tears.

"My parents were pacifists. They had protested the talk of war with Xian. My mother's brother, Singe Lin Minor, hated anything that was not Croffer. I listened to their conversations when I was supposed to be in bed. He claimed Xandavier was ours, not Xian's. That we were treated like second-class citizens. And Mother would ask him, 'How can it be our planet when they were there first for thousands of years?' Then he would storm off. Now, he's the leader of our people still spewing hatred."

She lifted his hand to her lips and kissed it tenderly. "If you will trust me, I need to go back and reveal this truth. So many will continue to die because of his misguided efforts. If it means my death or his, I still must go."

Tartar stood. "I just found you. How can I let you go? I trust you, my heart. I don't trust him. He is likely to kill you because you won't have Iona and Hester with you." Facing her, he fell to his knees. "It is because of you; I am who and what I should be. I've never known I was part dragon. And we, my dragon and I, cannot live without you. If you leave, we will die... and because we are Life-Mates, you will suffer, too. I can't bare for you to go through such pain."

"Tartar, *yenoh*, think about it. If the situation was reversed, wouldn't you go back by yourself to confront your demons so you could be free to love me?" He reluctantly nodded. "I need this too, to give all myself to you."

Fabric brushed against metal. *An assassin!* She moved to protect Tartar.

He put his hands on her shoulders and pointed to Xander with a smile.

Chuckling, she shook her head. These people were very touchy-feely. The noise had been Xander putting Iona, with Hester, on his lap.

"Hey, you don't have to protect me. I'm a big guy. Besides, these are my friends."

"Where I am from there are no such things as trusted friends, and an assassin could sneak in here to kill you. I won't take chances with your life."

Someone else was in the room. She couldn't see them, but she could feel their presence. *The vents. I used the vents. Only one other person knew that. He was the only capable of sneaking on board.*

She glanced at the vent near her. She couldn't see anything, and the baby wasn't being fussy.

Iona got off Xander's lap and handed Hester to him. "She's right, Tartar, and you know it. In her profession, they'll keep coming after her till they bring her back or kill her. What she needs is a new profession." Chith at first thought she was insane until she noticed everyone was shouting. Everyone, that is, except Saarn and Iona.

Chith stood and stepped toward Iona.

Singe Lin dropped from the top vent and landed between the two females. He grabbed Chith, put his fingers tips on both sides of her windpipe, as he hauled her back to his chest. "So, tell me what is this career change you want for my best asset? And why shouldn't I kill her right now? She betrayed me."

Xander stopped her when she turned to him and said, "Oline." He stepped back to let a calm Iona stand in front of Singe and put a hand on his arm.

"Tell me how she betrayed you? How long have you been up there listening? If your ears were working, you'd know she'd never do that to you. You are the one who betrayed her and so many others. How many other battles did you blame on our people when it was you? You killed your own people."

Singe Lin dragged Chith back a step. "I had too. Those in power at the time held my family. They weren't just going to kill them, they were going to torture them, including my infant daughters. It was the only way they would live."

Iona followed him. "Are they still the ones giving the orders? Or is it you?" She stared into his eyes. "Do you really want to live their lie? Or is it time for truth?"

His hand dropped from her throat. Chith faced him stoically. "Was it worth my family dying? And you say they held your family... what family? As far as I knew I was what was left of your family. I've never seen you or heard of you having a mate and younglings."

Singe's misery and horror stared out of his eyes. "They showed me a vid of where they held my family before the bombing. Then the authorities gave me footage of where everyone I loved being blown to bits. They told me there were no survivors. You were dead, my heart was ripped my body."

"In my fury," he snarled. "I launched fighters and bombers against our people."

Saarn leaned back in his chair. "What if your family never died? What if they were rescued?"

Singe moved so fast he was a blur, dropping Chith and yanking Saarn out of his chair, placing him in a chokehold. "What the *shite* do you mean? There were bodies found. Autopsies were performed to establish who they were. The DNA was theirs." He shook him, causing him to gag.

Saar moved his head and gestured to let him talk. "I know, because we don't kill innocents. I and Tartar went on King Niall's order to rescue them. Xander never knew. I can have them brought here to prove it. Oh, and they had plenty of time to pull DNA from them for tests while they were prisoners."

Singe

Could his family really be alive? Could all this violence finally end?

Two seconds later, Chith was at his side, her hand on his shoulder. "Singe, please, let them come. See for yourself. Don't take anyone's word."

He shook Saarn. "Have them come in. I know their markings and can separate them from others easily."

Hitting his com unit on his shirt, "Bring them in."

Ten mins later a knock came on the unit door. Xander yelled out, "Enter."

Three Croffer females and a male entered. The two middle-aged females led, one noticeably taller than the other, followed by an older female, possibly their mother, slightly stooped. All donned dark, unassuming garments, as though in mourning. Their foreheads and cheeks bore distinct markings. The shorter female sported delicate horns on her chin, while her taller companion had them at her temples. The elder showcased them at both her chin and temples. A male, about five years their junior, entered last. He stood tall, matching Singe's height, with markings gracing his cheeks and chin, and larger horns protruding from his temples and chin.

Seeing them Singe shouted. "What is this? You're lying. I had my mate and two daughters, no son."

The older female stopped mid-stride. "You would call your mate a whore? You would dare to suggest that he is not your son? We made him the night before they stole us from you. We have waited and waited for you, only to be greeted thusly?" She grabbed the others and was turning them around.

Singe dropped Saarn and stared at the small group. Had they made love? Yes, he'd never forget how they had loved. Even now he could feel her hands caressing his horns. He stretched out his hands, taking a step toward them. "Dila. My Dila. Please forgive me. I know you would never let another touch you. Why have you stayed here and not come to me or gotten word to me?"

She went to him like a mother duck, with her ducklings following. "How could we go to you? If they used us before, they would again." She glanced at Saarn. "He wanted us to let you know we were safe. I was terrified at what they would do to you and us. Back then, the leaders were eyeing our daughters and talking about taking my unborn from me."

"Who were they, Dila? Who threatened our children and you?"

Dila visibly trembled and seemed to shrink before his eyes. Their children ran to her, the girls hugging her and the son bringing a chair and blanket for her.

"What is wrong? Have I hurt you? I would cut off my arm rather than hurt you, Dila." He slowly crept forward till he could drop to his knees in front of her.

When the quivering stopped, "Your tone was just as theirs was. I have panic attacks when I hear it."

"When you can tell me, I will listen."

Before he could address his children, Chith couldn't contain herself. "All these years have been a lie. What you forced me to endure and learn things that were the opposite of what my parents wanted for me. Why? Why couldn't you have left me at that orphanage?"

"All of this is horrendous. I, too, have lost my parents, my sister... I have only Xander and Hester." Iona wiped the tears from her face. "What is more important than anything right now is not us as individuals but as nations. Can you, will you, put your personal feelings aside for a few minutes and listen to the job we have for you?"

Singe sat on the floor, holding Dila's hand, their children behind them. Chith sat down next to Tartar. Saarn stood to Iona's right, and Xander to her left.

Xander

Xander's gaze rested on each person. "I think this idea is perfect and will aid both our peoples enormously. I also believe there will be resistance, and security measures will need to be taken. Two nights ago, Iona had a dream. There was peace between us. Your people were on the planet Uli. It had been terraformed, so it was habitable. Something we couldn't do years ago. Singe and his family were the leaders. None of this surprised me. Not until she told me Chith was their ambassador to Xandavier and had mated Tartar. And Saarn was our ambassador to Uli, promised to Singe and Dila's oldest daughter, *Missine*."

Chith laughed. "Me, an assassin turned ambassador. No one will believe it." When no one else laughed, she gave them all a disbelieving glare. "Look at me. I've never had training for such."

Iona

"Oh, but you have. You negotiated with me, you might have lied, but you knew what to say to get me to do what you wanted me to. You were firm but not argumentative. Nothing pushy. Gentle nudges. You made me feel like you cared." Iona's reading of their lone conversation was astute.

Goddess, she's right. I did those things. Maybe I'm capable... she tilted her head at Tartar. "You'd be by my side?"

"I'd stick to you like glue."

Chapter 21

Later that Day

"Have you talked to Tartar about his wings? What did Healer Ranin say? I know today was the day to discuss it and it should probably just be the two of you… I'm so curious." Iona held Xander's hand and whispered to him as they made a dash to their suite.

"Yes, I talked with Ranin. He said it was done over three thousand years ago when our grandparents were on their ship in isolation. He believed it was airborne. And it was used to suppress the dragon part of our people's DNA. He thinks the people were told it was to protect them from a disease. It was the extreme stress Tartar was under that brought his dragon forth. And when he and Chith mate, she will become *Argonda*—dragon—like you did."

"Will she have wings? Or will she be wingless like me?" She could feel her dragon's heartbreaking, as she didn't have the freedom of Xander's.

"I discussed this with Ranin, too. His answer was that it would happen when your dragon's body was ready and not a day sooner. You cannot rush it. It could maim her."

"As for Tartar, he is ecstatic about the wings... and Saarn wants them too. You'd think they were in the toy store when they talked with Ragin. Almost jumping up and down with excitement."

See, I told you it will happen. We just need to be patient. Then we will fly beside our mates.

I hear. But want now. I patient, promise.

Iona's Surprise

Iona peered down the hall and smiled. The guards had seen them. They had the door open. Without missing a beat, they entered and heard the door close softly behind them as Iona jumped up into Xander's arms. Her legs were around his waist as she pulled her blouse loose, while his lips devoured hers. She pulled away slightly to take it off over her head, then she pressed her hands to the side and under her breasts, lifting them to his lips. She relished the warmth of his mouth sucking on her, and his hands working under her dress to reach her core. On top of that, she couldn't stop her hips from rubbing furiously against him.

Finally, his hands were fully under her skirt. She had purposely not worn any panties. He groaned when he dipped his fingers in her and spread the wetness from front to rear, circling her entrance each time. "Stop Xander. Let me down." Shocked at her demand, he let her slide down his front.

"You stay there. Don't move, except to take off those clothes." She winked and walked to the closet. She opened it and pulled out what looked like a footstool but wasn't. Its top was waist high to Xander. It had handles coming out of one side, and a step went at an angle underneath the wide seat. There were two cushions under the stool that were far apart and an extra deep seat. The handles were adjustable and had grips on them.

She dragged it over in front of him. Then she finished disrobing, then draped herself half over the wide seat of the stool. Her knees were tucked under it on the cushions, so her legs were spread wide. Her stomach didn't quite cover the top cushion. Iona's body was at an angle. Gripping the handles caused her breasts to perk up, exposing their puckered tips.

Xander didn't waste any time discussing. He had discarded his clothing and saw something hanging from the side of the stool. She had attached a bottle of love paste. Every place he put it would increase their pleasure. He'd never used it. His mate was adventurous. He quickly put some on his thick throbbing rod, then rubbed it from her clit to her tawny rose bud. He added a few more drops and reached forward to coat her nipples with it.

When he was finished, she was mewling with need. Arching her back, pushing herself toward him. He rubbed her back and nibbled her neck.

"Please Xander."

He stretched till he was nibbling between her shoulder and ear. Shaking, she didn't think she could take it anymore. She opened her mouth to plead when he was at her opening. He grabbed her breasts, plucking them, pulling her back to him, thrust into her to the hilt and bit her neck. She screamed, "YES!" Every time he pumped into her, his dragon buried its teeth in her neck, she climaxed. When he filled her with his seed, she was limp. He had to carry her to their bed.

Xander woke up to a soft, small hand clasping his engorged shaft and lips running over his shoulder. A silky leg slipped over his middle. Rolling on his back, he watched with slitted eyes as Iona scooted down and without a word took his shaft gently in her hands, lifting his swollen balls up. It felt so wonderful; he jerked when she licked him, then blew on the dampness. It was cool, but made his body burn; it took his breath away. After she did this, she moved up and took him deep into her mouth. Moving up and down. He placed his hands in her hair and guided her, as her hands continued to caress his balls.

He pulled her up. "No, my seed needs to be in you."

Her body flowed like a gentle breeze up his body. She nibbled on his chest up to his neck, lifting herself. She waited till he watched her join them together. It was the hottest thing he'd seen. He grasped her hips and moved them in time with his as she nibbled her way to his neck, rubbing her breast across his body. He couldn't contain himself. "I'm coming." She bit his neck with her dragon's teeth and came.

Xander rolled to his side, laying her next to him, and wrapped his arms around her.

He lifted one hand and smoothed her hair away from her face, leaned down and kissed her forehead, nose, chin, and lips with a tenderness he'd never shown before.

"Good morning my heart."

He rubbed his nose with hers. "Now, tell me where you got that chair and potion?"

"Well, I didn't know who to ask at first. I mean I've never talked to anyone about what we do." She felt heat rise to her face and figured she was beat red. "I decided if I was on earth, I would ask Dina or my gynecologist. Since we don't have that here, I asked Ranin. He was so nice, not embarrassed at all. He told me about the lotion, how it enhances both the male and female's pleasure, and where to procure it.' She buried her face in his chest. "As for the chair.... When I went in the store, I saw it. That's why I don't quite fit on it, and I saw the minute he realized it too. He offered to make a smaller one for me. I took him up on it, and asked him when it would be ready, so I could send someone to pick it up."

Xander gazed at her with a worried look. He saw Iona pull back. "Did I do something wrong?"

"Yes, no. Well, both I suppose. My heart, you're the Queen. To let the public know something so private is not always a good thing. It can turn into a scandal."

"Oh, I knew that. That's why I wore a heavy veil. He couldn't see my face, and none of my guards wore the royal crest. That's why I told him I'd send someone to pick it up. I paid for it then, too."

She paused.

"Plus, Captain Neor, said he put a listening device in the male's shop. All he heard was the male's comments that I was a strange one. But he was glad for the commission. It made it possible to pay his bills this month."

"I'm glad Noer thought to monitor him, and to not wear our crest. Because I am very surprised and happy."

Chapter 22

Royal Healer Alain S'Tryker's Quarters

Alain stepped out of his shower, stepped in front of the cleansing room mirror and admired himself, turning one way, then the other. He smiled and nodded. He was a wonderful specimen of a Xian male in his prime. Any female he chose should know she was privileged to be with him.

In fact, anyone who was around him or cared for by him was lucky.

He strode into his closet and pulled out his uniform and put it on when the voice spoke. *You are so pitiful and useless. Just as you cheated when you were youngling and becoming a grown male, you can't get by on just your looks or your parents' positions.* A hideous laugh filled his head. He grabbed his head with both hands and fell to the floor.

His eyes stared sightlessly at the walls until his com went off. "Royal Healer you are wanted in Medical."

He shook his head, glanced around, and responded, "I'll be there shortly."

Fear flooded his face as he glanced around before he left. *Why was I on the floor? That's the fifth time it's happened.*

When he reached Medical, all he needed was to sign off on some papers for supplies. *Why had they made it sound so important?*

That laugh echoed through his mind. He glanced around to see if anyone else had heard it. No reaction at all. Only him.

He headed toward his office, hah! He, the Royal Healer and Head Medical for Xandavier, was relegated to the basement. Not the spacious office Ranin had used when he was the Royal Healer... Nooo, he was still in it. Right next to the royal family's quarters. In fact, Alain wasn't allowed to touch the Queen or Princess... they hadn't let him examine the Croffer prisoner. The unmitigated gall. None of them realized what they had done by rejecting him.

He had a plan. They were going to learn he is the only one that can do the rejecting. Anyone who thought they were better than him deserved his correction. All his classmates learned the hard way. He guessed royalty wasn't any different from those idiots.

He'd show them. Those who knew how to heal also knew how to kill.

Chapter 23

Royal Healer Alain S'tryker

"How dare they?" Healer Alain S'tryker slammed his fist on his crappy desk. His office didn't have executive style furniture. Noooo, what they gave him befitted a lower-class receptionist. It was far beneath someone with his position and title. How dare they!

Surrounded by his many sacrosanct who tutted as he flexed his hands. He'd hit the useless piece of trash hard enough to put a dent in it. Good, he hadn't broken his hand.

Two of his minions approached him, offering to treat his bruises. He let them touch him. He could read in their faces how honored they felt to aid him.

Why was no one else from Medical or the Officer Corp down here? It was just him and his followers.

No patients. He was the Royal Healer. He was the highest trained medical person in Xandavier, and no one would use his skills, all because of that *betch*. Everything had changed after Xander brought her and the child on board.

She wasn't worthy or fit to be queen. The child he would deal with, but that female, she needed to go... and never come back.

Ranin should be banned, not retired. Alain had studied harder than anyone else to become the Royal Healer. He experimented and taught himself what he needed to know. They had no right to deny him. He set up his own experiments. He'd figured out how to use nanites for healing among other things. Of course, he had to first cut his volunteers to see if it would work or not. But that's what you needed the guts to do.

Those who volunteered to help him further his medical studies signed a non-disclosures and papers saying they couldn't refuse any test he did on them. Of course, he had to get those of his people who had nothing and lived wherever they could. None had relatives, so if something failed and they died, he'd do the death certificate and slip in with the other papers his instructions never read, just signed.

He had heard his entire lifetime that Xian could transform into dragons. He tracked every cell of his patient's DNA. None had anything that would show a whole other being as part of them. Since he couldn't find anything to substantiate their ability to transform into dragons, he knows it was fables to tell children. Not a bit of truth. Any time he tried to show his finding, the senior Healers would tell him he didn't know what he was looking for. He knew it was lies, all lies and myths.

Everyone would know he was right. He would prove to the world, he and he alone, was the slayer of myths. He would prove he was right.

Crazy rumors of dragons. None have been around for over thousands of years. What nonsense.

The sound of feminine laughter filter into his office. He shuttered. Only two adult females on this ship, but he'd recognize the Queen's laugh anywhere. He nodded to his followers and headed out of Medical away from the laughter.

Ranin Seeks Alain

Ranin bowed to Iona, "Highness, I'll be right back. I want to ask Healer Alain something. He specialized in the genetics of our people. He would have some answers I need."

Ranin walked into Alain's area to find it empty and the edge of a coat from one of his followers flapping as he ran off. *Damn. Alain must be really hurt and angry.*

When Alain was a student, if he felt his classmates were teasing him or ridiculing him, somehow those students got hurt. Teachers found drugs in one's locker. Another was told his family would have to pay... his younger sister was beaten, and gang raped. Another was caught with a test key sheet and expelled for cheating. Oh, had he heard Alain laughing at each incident? One or two suddenly quit their training. They'd come to him quietly later and shared how Alain had threatened them and their siblings. He had a hard time believing them, but now? Now, he had this petty attitude, acting like no one wanted him to treat them when it was so far from the truth.

He knew Alain was feeling humiliated. What was he plotting? It must be against the King and Queen.

He took a second to calm himself before departing to return to the Queen. He didn't want the Queen to be frightened by seeing him unsettled.

"Highness, he's not here, Highness. I'll try to catch him later."

Alain's Treachery

Hallway door into the Royal Suite's private kitchen. Alain softly knocked on the door. "Just a moment. I'll be right there." The male under-chef called out.

When he opened the door, Alain presented two small bottles to her. "I have something for the King and Queen. Healer Ranin contacted me earlier. He told me they needed one of my elixirs. But the Queen still refuses to see me. So, I need you to take this to their cook, tell her it needs to be served in a glass on ice as a bedtime cocktail." Alain smiled as he handed the two bottles to his top aide. "Thank you, Usef."

Grinning, he went back to Medical, where his minions were waiting for his instruction.

He faced his faithful followers. "It's quiet and all the emergency stations are manned. Take the day off. I'll keep my com unit on for any emergencies. You've all worked hard and deserve a break." He waved them off with a smile.

When the last one could no longer be seen, Alain commed Healer Pinder, his number one, his chief confidant. "Meet me in my room. My plan has been set in motion."

He glanced around. No one was watching. He silently slipped out of Medical and headed to his quarters. He couldn't keep the grin off his face. This plan was perfect. He would make them pay. He skipped a few steps when a warrior walked by staring at him, then shaking his head, he swallowed his glee so no one would suspect.

I must be careful my happiness doesn't show. The people don't know how wonderful it will be to not to deal with royalty—only me. I have so many ideas for our people and world. I know they will love them as much as I do. And if they don't... Well, they'll just have to leave or die.

Healer Pinder

Pinder told Alain he was on his way. Then he commed Ranin. "Sir, he's got something planned and told me to meet him in his room. He said his plan has been set in motion."

"Be very careful, Pinder. He is smart and sly. As soon as you discover the plan, contact me so I can warn the King and Queen."

Alain may have been confiding in Pinder, but the reverse was not true. Pinder admired Healer Alain's education and knowledge when it came to medicine. He had no time for his political plots within plots. Alain made them so intricate that he couldn't keep track of what the plan was.

Pinder was waiting when Alain arrived at his door. "Good, you are here. Now we won't have to wait to get started." He rubbed his hands together with a vicious smile.

"Sir, what are we starting?"

"Not here. Inside."

Using his palm to open his door, Healer Alain led the way into his quarters. They were huge compared to Pinder's. Alain liked to rub it in, he always said his were nicer than the king's. Of course, none of his followers had ever been in the royal suite, but he had. Their furniture was something he'd put in a country cottage and worn from the years it has been in their family. Their rooms sometimes were a mess. Nothing was as new and sharp as his. He was the one living like a King, whereas their King was living like a pauper.

This time, Alain didn't waste any time with niceties. He sauntered across to the large screen. "On screen. 'Wake up plan.'"

Schematics showed up on the screen with the king and queen's names, dates, times, and their current locations on it. Pinder moved swiftly to his side. Looking at it more closely, whatever this was, it was to take place tonight and tomorrow.

Crap. How did I miss this?

How am I going to get word to the Ranin?

If he tried to leave now, he was dead. He'd peered into his superiors' eyes before Alain turned away. They were wild. All restraint was gone.

"Royal Healer Alain, what would you have me do? Is there some way I can help you ensure this plan goes smoothly?" *Maybe he'll send me to do a chore, and I can get in touch with someone in the Elite Guard.*

"Yes, Healer Pinder. Your assignment is to get the override code from security. Don't look so aghast. I've arranged for it to be ready for you. Do change into something that doesn't shriek medical clothing. I don't want them to know where you work. Go requisition some new clothing... better yet, do that first. Pick something you'd wear taking a female to dinner."

He nodded enthusiastically. Afraid that if he opened his mouth, he would scream. *'You haven't even thought this through. You are an idiot. We're going to die.'*

Alain wore a smug smile in place of his usual sour expression. He waved Pinder off as he sang in a sing-song voice. "You got yours, I get mine, ta da ta do, I win each time." Then giggled.

Pinder wanted to see what had happened before he met with Alain and see what he was up to after he left, but he was only one deep. Healer Ranin knew how vicious Alain could be... none of the times before had he looked so scary, and Alain wasn't even going after him.

When Pinder arrived at the requisition office, the first thing he noticed when he entered was a camera monitoring anyone who did business there. He approached the clerk. "I'm here to pick up some new clothing, formal wear."

"Sure, no problem, but they won't be ready for two *hurs*. Come back then." The clerk nodded to the male behind him and said, "Next."

Scurrying to his room, he was drenched in sweat; he needed a shower. And he gazed at his com device, that wouldn't do. A secure line was required for this. Where could he get one? Outside his cleansing room, he could hear his com unit buzzing.

Running, he snatched it off the dressing table.

"Yes," came out in a near shout.

"Pinder, why didn't you answer sooner?"

He closed his eyes and prayed for calmness. "Healer Alain. I had forgotten it in my quarters. And I went to order the clothing first. They will be ready in two *hurs.*"

The glee in his superior's voice overrode any other emotions, making Pinder sick. "Rest up. We're going to be very busy tonight. I can't guarantee any rest."

As soon as they were disconnected, Pinder ran to Ranin's rooms next to the Royal Suite. No one was there. He went to the secure com device on his desk and prayed he did it right. *Please pick up.... Come on answer. We've got to stop him"*

"Hello. This is Healer Pinder. I'm trying to reach Healer Ranin. Can you fetch him for me?"

"Healer Ranin, you say."

"Yes, it is very important."

He heard a chair scrape across a wood floor, footsteps.

"This is Healer Ranin."

"Sir, this is Pinder. He has something planned for tonight. I'm supposed to pick up the override key for all rooms. I'm in your quarters because I don't know if he bugged mine." Pinder couldn't quit talking. "He met with some medics before I met with him...

"I'm not sure what they are supposed to do. Oh, and he said there might not be any sleep tonight. We've got to warn the King."

"Don't you worry, Pinder. Everything will be taken care of. The King is being warned as we talk."

"Thank you. I must go, so he doesn't know."

"You do that. I'll see you later."

Chapter 24

Castle's Fencing Practice Rooms

Fury poured off Alain as he walked into the room, stopping at the edge of the marked off practice area. He nodded at his opponent, Pinder, who was already wearing his mask. His betrayer.

He'd been questioning Ranin and punishing him any time he didn't answer correctly when Ranin's com unit had gone off. He'd lowered his voice and listened to Pinder report to Ranin what his plans were. How dare he. Pinder's betrayal meant he had to die. And this was the perfect way to take care of it. Accidents happened during such training.

They moved to the center, saluted with their swords, then Alain swung his rapier at his opponent with all his anger, who deflected him. Both were dressed in fencing protection garb, and protective tips were on the points of their blades. Alain stepped back and swung his blade back and forth, then went to the en'garde position. His opponent joined him in the center of the room. When he disengaged from en'garde, he purposely scraped his tip off. His minions around him started shouting, to call the match and put down their swords, that his tip was off.

He was deaf to their cries.

The male he was battling was weakening. He didn't see a male in a protective suit any longer. It was Pinder, the traitor.

The voice egged him on. *How dare he think he could inform Ranin about you. I've told you over and over, I'm the only one you can trust. Kill him!*

I will, because he was such a fool he didn't even know it was me he tattled to.

It chuckled. Remember you are in charge, not the King or Queen. Destroy the foolish traitor like you will the King and Queen. If he wants to follow them, let them lead him to Hadias' firey pit.

Alain fainted to the right. As his opponent recovered, he stabbed him in the center of the chest. *Gods that felt good, he had no right to live.* Glee filled Alain as the traitor fell to the floor, his rapier sticking out of him. Still convinced he was fighting Pinder a sense of satisfaction filled him. With a flourish, he knelt beside the betrayer and tore the mesh mask from his face.

Stumbling to his feet, he stared in horror. *It was his half-brother, Mevon. This can't be! It was supposed to be Pinder; I was fighting not my Mevon. He wasn't even supposed to be here. He was the best little brother...He was my number one fan. What would their Bormah and Monah say? He had to let them know it was Pinder's fault.*

Alain surveyed his minions, then back at his brother, cried out. "Fracke you, Pinder. This is all your fault. You killed Mevon. You're next you bustard."

Wiping his sword, he entreated each of those watching. "This is Pinder's fault for being a traitor. He will pay for it with his life. But first we need to pay homage to my brother. We'll take him to Medical, there we'll prepare his body."

The emergency team arrived and removed the body. Alain followed them to Medical... he didn't realize out of the twelve original followers, only four went with him. The others scattered like leaves in the wind.

The Royal Suite

"Xander?" Iona called from their sitting room. "Can you come here?"

All she heard in reply was running feet. She was at the doorway, looking in on Hester. She lifted a finger and covered her mouth, then pointed inside the room.

Hester was hanging on to furniture as she walked about her room with a smile of triumph. On her second circuit, she started talking to everything she touched, as if she was saying "thank you" for helping her. She turned toward them unexpectedly and bellowed out "Mama. Papa. See!"

Rushing into her room giving her praise for such a smart girl. Xander tossed her into the air as she giggled and drooled. Iona quickly grabbed a cloth diaper and wiped his shirt as they both laughed.

Iona's brow scrunched together. "I can't believe she talks, walking and drooling with her new teeth. We need to watch her; she could develop a fever with so much happening in her little body."

"My love, you are probably right, but I think right now the results are exhaustion." They both laughed as she yawned, her red-rimmed eyes at half-mast. She grinned, dropped her head on Iona's shoulder fast asleep.

There was a gentle knock on the door from the kitchen staff area. Iona laid Hester down and covered her, then followed Xander to see who it was. Neither had asked for a snack tonight.

Halfway across the room Xander called out, "Come in."

"Arret, what have you there?"

Their maid had a silver tray with two iced drinks on it. "Majesty, I don't know what it is. One of them medics brought it earlier and said Healer Ranin had ordered it as a nightcap for the two of you. He said you was to drink it all up."

"Thank you Arret. Leave the tray with the drinks. We'll do as Healer Ranin asks." He dismissed her with a nod.

Together, they went into their room. Xander brought the tray with him and set it on the desk. Iona was still brushing her hair in the cleansing room, as Xander lifted a glass to his lips.

At her scream, "NO!" He stopped and set it back down. She ran to him. "Did you drink any of that?"

"No, but why don't you want me to? It is from Ranin. He would never harm us."

"No, he wouldn't, but someone acting in his name could. Think about it. When has he ever sent someone with something for us? Never. Why would he start now? And on top of that, I haven't been able to get hold of him all day. I've been waiting because I know he takes care of some of the people who have no money."

"Why didn't you say something earlier?"

"I thought he was in the village. And didn't want to be that demanding queen. I so appreciate what he is doing for our people there."

She went to him and wrapped her arms around him. Then she plucked a glass from the tray and smelled it. One seemed fuller than the other; there was more ice in one. She smelled the one she held that had little ice. It was so gross. Setting it down with a shudder, she picked up the other and sniffed. That smelled wonderful. She almost wanted to gobble it up. In a flash, she ran to the cleansing room facilities and tossed it down and flushed. She waved to Xander to bring the other one, and it met the same fate as the first.

Taking the glasses to the sink, she was going to rinse them when Xander's hand stopped her.

He leaned over shoulder, acting like he was kissing her neck. "We need to test it. And I'm pretty sure if they knew how to get this to us, they could have bugged our suite. Act like everything is normal."

Using his normal tone, he added, "Humm that was good. Come, my love. Tomorrow is going to be a big day, and I want to snuggle with you."

Once they were in bed, Xander pulled the covers over their heads, muffling their voices. "Xander, why do you think our rooms are bugged?"

"I not sure, it is a gut feeling. There is something here that is irritating my dragon. It's almost as if he can't settle."

"I believe we can sense when we are being spied on. It is so different from just being out and about and the people coming at us with their cameras. Who would do something like that?"

"Off the top of my head, I would say it was Healer Alain. Your refusal of his services caused others who knew about it to refuse his services, as well."

"I'm calling Tartar and Saarn," he added. "I'm pretty sure they haven't finished packing; they haven't completed their day's duties. They'll understand immediately who's at the crux of the whole thing."

Iona laid her head on his shoulder. "When do you think they will come?"

He lifted her chin with this finger. "I would say *half hur* to a *hur*. Whoever is behind this will want to make sure we are incapacitated."

He turned off the lights. "I'm going to go get my armor on and grab my weapons. Can you reach your knife?"

At her nod he reminded her, "If needed go for the eyes. They will kill you no matter what they say."

Back in bed he placed his spare armor over her chest, then pulled the bedcovers up. He whispered, "You can pull them up to over your face."

Two minutes later, Iona tugged on his hair, and whispered, "I hear scratches behind the headboard."

Nodding, he pushed his covers off, slipped out of bed, then put his pillows where his body was. Iona did the same. She slid under the bed, while he stood by the headboard behind the bed curtains.

A cold musty breeze moved the dust ruffle slightly, kicking up enough fine particles that Iona had to hold her nose shut. There must be a secret passage behind the wall where the bed was shoved up against. There was a low light coming in through the doorway. She counted six sets of boots. The only thing that held her in place was Xander saying he would be distracted if she entered the battle. She was to wait for Tartar and Chith.

The door to their bedroom burst open. With the light behind them, their silhouettes told them who they were. Reinforcements.

The three were immediately engaged. She heard a familiar voice yelling, "Kill them all!"

Alain!

Oh no, everyone in the Castle had heard about the not-so-secret door in the closet. I must secure it. He might get away, and he's the type who won't give up.

She was learning he was vicious and unbalanced. He needed to be protected from himself and other... patting her knife in her robe pocket, she'd use it if she had to.

Sliding out from under the bed, she crept over to her side chair. Praying for strength, she lifted the chair placing it right in front of the exit to the passageway. She stood still along the wall. The flash of sparks that came from swords meeting in battle lit up the room, followed by grunts and groans. Mixed in with the clashing sounds, she heard footsteps of someone untrained in stealth, heading back to the way they came in. She glanced around for something large and strong. But not too heavy. She didn't want to use her knife. Ah, her favorite metal vase. That's exactly what she needed.

Whoever it was hit the chair. "Oh no you don't." She lifted her vase high over her head and brought it down on his head as he tried to untangle himself from the chair he had toppled over. When he fell, she yanked free the curtain ropes and used them to hog-tie him.

She was staring at him, trying to figure out who he was when the lights went on. It was Healer Alain. *What the ....*

Tartar came and dragged him back into the bedroom with the others.

She ran to Xander to make sure he was unharmed. What a mess. Bodies were strewn over furniture, crumpled on the floor and sitting holding wounds, with eyes filled with shock. Thank goodness no one was dead.

Alain spit at Xander's feet. "She is not a fit queen. You'll see. She is not who you think she is."

Ignoring Alain, Xander went to Noer, then waved Tartar and Chith over. "Find out if there are any more like them. I want them all gathered up."

Two guards were escorting Alain out when Saarn came in with a battered and bruised Ragin. He stopped and looked Alain up and down. "Was your treachery worth it?"

The rest of the elite guards followed Tartar and Chith, removing the rest of the attackers to the detention cells... each one that was part of the attack was a medic. People pledged to heal.

Iona stood back with Xander as they left. *What a waste of training and skill. Would ever want a Healer that will kill?*

Chapter 25

The Aftermath

Iona ran to Ranin, quickly guided him to a chair. "My friend. I wouldn't want anything like this to happen to you. I know we only have you as a Healer …"

"Highness, I sensed something was wrong and spoke to the King. I've started the clearance process, with the King's permission, on two healers coming from the provinces of Sumtin, near our eastern ocean. They are twins, Jazzo Ceter and his sister, Mintry. She is our first female Healer."

Giving him a big hug, she sent a telepathic message to Xander. *Thank you.*

Hester started crying in her room. Iona hurried into her, changed her diaper, and brought her out with her bottle. Ranin was talking to Xander.

"... He has lost his mind completely. I've heard of people who are incredible smart, are also very weak in their minds. They can't relate to the people they are treating. Unfortunately, they think of them as test subjects. Sire, I would like to have one of our top psychologists examine him before any judgment is issued."

"Oh, I agree Ranin. But I think Iona was the last straw. There were too many things happening at once. More changes than he could handle. What I'm curious about is when did it begin?"

"Your Majesty, I think it started as a young male. He couldn't abide being teased, and I've found out just how horrendous his revenge was for it. Everything from hiring someone to hurt a fellow student or a family member, to stealing something to plant on another student. He was so good at hiding it. I didn't know how bad it was until the Queen asked me to come out of retirement that it became apparent."

"I see. It started long ago. He is very sick. He couldn't retaliate against a queen the way he could his coworkers or subordinates. I believe that pushed him over the edge. We need to know just how badly he had slipped. Only a professional will be able to determine that. And tell us if he is competent to stand trial."

A huge gurgle came from the rocking chair where Iona was giving Hester her food. Iona jumped up from the chair, handed the baby to Xander, and ran from the room with one hand on her mouth and the other on her stomach.

Xander, half stood when Ranin's hand touched his arm, and he shook his head. "Give her some privacy. She's battled and done things she's never had to do. It is probably shock setting in. I will check on her later today. I think all of us need to leave you three alone."

"Call if you need me." Ranin stood and moved as fast as male half his age.

"Wait, did you get your questions answered about our people's dragon DNA?"

"Yes, Sire. It is still fully in us; we have to learn how to access it."

Ragin took a step toward the door when Xander asked. "When are the new healers due in?"

"In three hurs, they are coming by *hujet*."

"Good, tell them I'll meet them at four in Medical. That should give them time to find their rooms."

"Yes, your Majesty." As Ranin left, Xander could hear retching in the other room. *Hum, never heard shock doing that to someone.*

Xander got a picture of Iona throwing up. It was Hester who showed him. He and Iona were going to have to teach Hester not to show such things to anyone else.

By time Iona came out of the bathroom, Xander was sound asleep on the sofa with Hester sleep-drooling all over his chest. How she wished she had a camera... *this was the king the people needed to see.*

Instead of looking for one, she curled up around them both and fell asleep, exhausted from the vomiting.

New Healers

It seemed like she had just fallen asleep when she heard a noise in their kitchen. Whoever it was, wasn't trying to be quiet. She sat up, put her hand over Xander's mouth, and shook him awake. Raising an eyebrow, she nodded her head toward their kitchen.

Xander whispered. "You take Hester, I'll investigate,"

Iona slipped from the couch and took Hester from him. The sounds of a pan being put on a stop top, then water from the tap, and a lid put on the pan. Footsteps came toward the door.

She mouthed, "I love you," to him as he silently crept to the door. The door slammed into his nose, and a large female came out holding a tray of food.

"Oh Sire. Highness. I didn't know you were awake yet. I thought I'd have something ready for you to eat before you woke up."

Xander touched his emergency com pinned to his left shoulder.

The sound of doors being flung open and warriors running in full gear filled the room. At the doorway, they came to a quick halt. Seeing no battle or threat, they saluted Xander.

"Sire, is there a problem?"

His gaze went from the Elite guard members to the woman standing with a calmness that couldn't be faked.

"Who is she? Why is she here?"

All eyes went to the female. She was average height for a Xian female, a little fuller figured but not overweight. Her hair was long and black, reaching below her hips. She had slippers on and a flower ankle tie. Something niggled at Iona. She was like the pictures she had seen of the island people in the Pacific from Earth before the meteor.

Before the guards could answer, two young people came in through the front door. "Ah, mamam, you fixed them something nutritious just as we asked.

You can go back to your kitchen, if you don't mind. We'll make sure they eat, then we'll do an exam. We'll check the baby first, so you can love her up while we do the other two. Okay?"

Iona clutched Hessie to her chest with one arm and waved her knife at them with the other. Xander's weapons were in his hands, and he'd stepped between Iona and Hessie and the strangers.

Captain Noer swallowed. "Sire, these are Healer Alain's replacements recommended by Healer Ranin. He escorted them here to introduce them to you and us. He said you were resting, but to let them stay."

"Noer, you're saying they have been checked and verified by security along with an in-depth review by you?"

"Yes, Sire. Healer Ranin had told me they were coming shortly after Queen Iona and Princess Hester refused to be treated by Healer Alain. He said they were the backup if there was no change between the healer and them."

Xander relaxed his stance and put his weapons away. "I remember now."

He faced Iona and took Hester from her. Together, they faced the strange female and the two younger people. "I knew that there was no chance you would change your mind about Alain, so I told Ranin to take care of it."

Noer took one step into the room. "Sire, let me introduce to you Staris Ceret, her two children who are healers, Jazzo and Mintry."

Staris curtsied and spoke to the room at large. "Sure, my babies. I fix a good meal and give that baby lots of love."

"Sire, if you'll sit here and put your head between your knees." Xander stared at him, realizing at the same moment his nose was bleeding.

"We'll get that bleeding under control. I'm Jazzo and this is my sister Mintry. While we take care of you, Mintry will check out the princess."

Mintry lifted Hester from Iona's arms, sat down with her, and did a quick exam. "She is such a beautiful child. And so smart. Mamam, would you come and collect the child?"

The kitchen door opened and Staris soundlessly walked in. "I'm here. Where is the little beauty?" She ambled over to her daughter, lifted Hester and took off with her into the kitchen. They could hear, "Ah, those new teeth hurt, huh? Let me give you something to chew on that will make them feel better."

Xander was now sitting up. His nose had stopped bleeding, and Mintry was talking to Iona in a low voice. He couldn't hear anything they said. Until Iona said, "You'll have to tell him soon. You can't hide this."

What is the world? She'd never tried to hide anything from him. He pushed Jazzo aside and knelt by Iona's side. "What is wrong, my heart? You can tell me."

Iona nodded to the kitchen at the twins. When they left, she took both Xander's hands in hers. She gave him a shy look, then down at her lap, and back at his face. "Hester is going to have a brother or sister in about seven months."

He gave her a look of incomprehension. "Hester can't have a brother or sister. Her parents…" She laughed as his mouth dropped open, then snapped shut. "How did this happen?"

"Oh, I would say the normal way." She rubbed her hands against the front of his pants.

"We're going to have a baby???"

"Yes."

Four heads peeked around the kitchen door. "Well, about that." Mintry cleared her throat. "The scan just finished giving me its full results. You are pregnant with more than one. I want you to come to Medical so we can verify it."

"No. I'm not going anywhere to verify anything. I am going to focus on my family. Hester and Xander… then the people of this world. If I am only two months along, a lot can happen between now and delivery. And you two have a lot to learn about human birthing... that is, unless you know a lot about it?"

"Um, no, your highness. We've studied childbirth with our species and the Croffers, but since we've never encountered another species...." They both lifted their hand palm up and shrugged their shoulders.

"I want one of you to go to Earth and take a crash course in obstetrics and gynecology. On earth they are called OB/GYN doctors. One needs to stay here. Either way, things will be different because we've only had one hybrid baby, Hester. I don't want the public told, either." With a sharp glance at Xander. "If something should happen in the next seven months where something goes wrong, no finger is to point at anyone. Understand?"

I wish my mom were here. We had talked about her being in the delivery room if ever I married and had a child. And Dina had said she would be with me too. Now they're gone.

Iona blinked, bringing herself back to what she was telling them saying she would tolerate.

"Now, I will agree to monthly checks, then biweekly and then weekly. It is normal for humans. No one is to know the gender or how many. Now, please have your mother come back in."

Mintry went to the kitchen and brought her in.

"Staris, who delivered your children?"

Staris smiled. "You know that answer. I did. No Healer was near us when they were born. Now, I help young mothers through their time of need."

"I remember my sister telling me that when I was born, they were up in the mountains and mom's, sorry Monah's labor was so fast, she couldn't reach a doctor. Our dad, Bormah, and my sister Dina delivered me. So, I am very grateful that you will be here to help."

"Your Bormah and sister were very brave."

"I think so too, and I miss them so much, especially now."

"On my planet we did have women, er females, that do what you do, we call them midwives. They deliver the baby, and if it is needed, a Healer is called. You shall be my midwife."

"I need to rest now." Her voice raised, "Xander, you need to catch me." He caught her just before she hit the floor. His dragon didn't wait, wings sprung out and before anyone could blink, he was in their bedroom, laying her down.

Six Months Later

Tartar had gotten a copy of the entrance exam so she could study it and be accepted. Mintry, passed as a human, fast-tracked the classes on earth. Iona had heard she would be returning in one *dat*. About time. She knew from when she was a child, multiple births were normally early. She was eight months along, and not a twinge yet. Staris was giving her worried looks. Every day they walked the hallways. Last month they had let the people know another baby was being born in the palace. The people and newscasters were running betting pools on the date and time.

Iona couldn't see her feet, and when the babies kicked, they knocked her off-balanced, sending her flying. Staris had started her on gentle chair exercises, along with walking for thirty mins in the morning and afternoon. Her back hurt, her stomach hurt and bones in her pelvic area were so painful, she wanted to cry. They moved her to a room with a toilet right next to the bed.

Xander still slept with her, if he wanted to call it that. He spent most of each night rubbing her back. Everyone, from the maid who cleaned up the dishes to people she'd never met were fussing over her. She could only sit or stand for so long, and the pain in her crotch was agonizing. Staris was telling her to lie on her side, when in walked Mintry.

She bypassed her mother's greeting when she witnessed the tears falling from her patient's eyes. "What's this crying? Let me help you." At her nod, Mintry pulled a hypo shot out of her bag and administered it to her hip.

Xander had been watching from the other room. "What is causing her so much pain that is not related to the delivery?"

"I saw something similar to this on Earth. The baby weighed too much for the mother. It was causing her pelvic bone to split. We need to rig a sling from the ceiling to hold her in the air. The main part needs to be around her hips. Hopefully, this will help her go full term with the pregnancy. The premature delivery can affect the lives of the little ones." She snared Xander's gaze. "We have an hour, then that sedative will wear off. Get your engineers and builders moving."

Staris put a handout and stopped her. "Did I do something that would hurt our Queen and the babies? I thought the walk with help." Tears filled her eyes.

"Mamam, you did the right thing. This is not normal. The babies, they have on earth are huge or tiny. The medical community believes it is something in that asteroid belt that hit their world. This is now common there."

One Month Later
Xander

"Mamam, make sure there is a chair in the shower for her highness, then get out of there. The King is to bathe her today." Mintry and her mother chuckled at each other as she flew out of the cleansing room.

"Sire, you can take her in now." She and her mother stayed in the anteroom with the door slightly open in case he needed them.

"Ah, my heart, why are you crying? Today the baby is due. You know I don't care if it is a boy or girl."

"Oh, Xander, it's not that. I look so terrible. I have stretch marks all over, and my breasts look like balloons."

He sat her on the chair. "That is what you may see, but not what I see. I see the marks on your body are badges of honor to me, that you cared enough to give us young. Your large breasts contain the nourishment our children will need to survive. You are perfect for me."

He turned on the water, washed her hair, then continued down to her toes when he felt her jerk. "Did I hurt you?"

Shaking her head, she said nothing, but rubbed her lower back. "Ok, I'll turn off the water and get you dry and back in bed. Maybe this was too much excitement."

The water went off. He enveloped her in a big fluffy bath sheet. She stood within his arms. He quickly got out and grabbed his bath sheet. As he reached for her, water gushed down between her legs. "Mintry get in here now."

Mintry

Two seconds later Mintry examined the fluid. "Yes, it is her water." She called out to her mother, "Mamam, contact Jazzo to assemble the team and start filling the tub with warm water."

Xander looked at her as if she was a battle commander. "Sire, remember, she wanted a water birth. It has proven good for mother and child. Less stress. Which means everyone needs to be in swimwear. You need to be next to her, and she won't be comfortable if you aren't covered. We have a special drape for her. "

She hadn't looked anywhere but his face. He smiled. "I'm wearing swim pants; I came prepared in case this happened."

"Oooooh, oooooh. I want to push."

Iona's hands clenched and her face scrunched up. *I must look like I'm constipated.*

"Don't push yet, Highness. I need to examine you and see how far you are along."

She then turned her face to the door and yelled. "Mamam, get in here."

"Highness, please, you need to pant. Look at Mamam and do what she does."

"Noooo. I can't, I can't stop. If I don't push, I'll explode!"

Mamam kneeled in front of Iona. "Highness pant with me. You can do it. Pant."

Mintry glanced up. "King Xander, carry her to the tub."

Mintry admired the tub. And observed the King sit his mate on the seat under the water. It was so nice to have basically a swimming pool for a bathtub. She pushed a button on the side and Iona's hips rose partially out of the water. Mintry placed her feet in strips, pushed her legs apart. "I'm going to touch you with my fingers to see how far you are dilated. Remember to do what Mamam does, pant and squeeze the King's hand."

Mintry sat up, lowered her patient's hips. "You are six *centi*. We can't have you pushing yet. It is too soon. Continue to pant and squeeze your mate's hand. It won't be long."

Mintry head back a snicker as she watched Iona leaned her head back and tilted it to one side so she could see Xanders face. "Next time you get to carry the babies. You hear me?"

Ten mins later Mintry grabbed a towel to dry her wet face and when she put it down, she saw Iona pushing. She quickly did an examination. "You are ten *centi*. I can feel the head. This next time I want to you grab your legs and push with all you have. It's okay if you curl up out of the water."

Mintry did a quick glance around the tub. Everyone was in position. "Heads up everyone. One, two, three. PUSH. Push... push — BREATHE."

"The head is crowning, here it comes. Give me another big push, and the head will be born." As Mintry was saying push, everyone joined in, cheering her on.

"The head is born, King Xander you need to come next to me. You are to sever the cord from the mother and release the baby into the world." She handed him the scissors and whispered, "Sire, you can do it."

"Last big push, Queen Iona. PUSH! You did good. She is beautiful. You have a beautiful daughter." She guided Xander's hand to the correct place to cut the cord.

She grinned at him. "If you like you can show her to her mother."

As soon as he showed her their baby daughter, Mintry started another exam to see how many more were in position. She popped her head up between Iona's knees. Nodded two times to Jazzo.

As soon as Iona held her daughter, a pain hit her worse than before. She raised frightened eyes to Mintry. "It's all right. It's the next baby. There are two more that I could find, three in total."

Grateful wasn't the word when the last one was born. Only it wasn't three, it was four. One girl and the rest were all boys. Both the King and Queen gazed in awe at the bassinets surrounding their bed.

Iona whispered to Xander, "Please I need to speak to Mintry, Jazzo, and Staris."

All three entered the bedroom and bowed. "Majesty, you wished to see us?"

"Yes, I wanted you to know from me personally how dear you three have become to us. You could have refused." The three objected. "Yes, I know you could have. I reached out to Ranin. I wanted more of your background. And he told me only what I already knew from our first meeting. That you cared, you have a deep compassion for all the people you have ever encountered. Their needs superseded your own. These are things you learned from your heart and parents.

"We needed you to hear it from us. We count you three, not only as our Royal Healers, but as friends and family. Thank you. I don't think our babies and I would have made it without your help. May God Selenia and Goddess Oline bless you and your family for ten generations."

Chapter 26

Names and Introductions

The four newborn babies woke up Hester, which had her crying for something to eat. And she wanted to know who they were and why they cried. Iona gave a sigh of relief when eight nursemaids came in. One carried clean clothing and diapers, the other had bottles of food. Rather than her trying to nurse them all, she had told Mintry she would express it so it could be shared between the babies.

All the nursemaids took the babies into the next room.

"We did it."

"No, my heart. You did it. You did all the work and created a family for us." Xander leaned down and kissed her. "Tomorrow is my turn. I get to introduce them to our world, along with the date and time they were born. Someone is going to win big."

"But we don't have names yet."

"How about family names? My brother named Hester after our mother. We can name our next daughter after your sister, Dina. The boys can be Naill, Manier," she put her hand on his arm and whispered, "Ranin. If it weren't for him.... I don't know what I would have done."

"Ranin, it is."

Younglings and Dragons

"The High Priest is here. Are all the younglings in the right blankets and is Hester dressed?" Iona was about to pull her hair out. She was still feeling puffy and fluffy, nothing fit.

"Everyone stand still for a minute." Mintry had entered the living room. She bowed to the Priest and curtseyed to the royal couple. "The Queen could hemorrhage if she stands the length of time I was told she would be. She needs a wheelchair and robes befitting the situation."

Staris had followed Mintry in. "All nursemaids line up with your charges. Princess Hester's maid and guards?" They went to stand at the back. "No, you come right after the parents. According to protocol, Priest first, parents, oldest youngling, then down to youngest. Of the new born, Dina, then Naill, Manier, and Ranin. Everyone is single file. Warrior Naing, you must keep a close eye on Hester, she's into climbing and that balcony is going to be tempting."

The High Priest went to Iona. "Highness, may I hold each of the younglings? I do not want them to be frightened of me. Seeing all the people while a stranger holds them might make them afraid."

"I think that is an excellent idea."

A knock sounded on the door and Tartar stuck his head in. "Majesties, it is fever pitch outside. They want to see the first ever quadruplets."

"Lead the way."

Iona was extremely happy that Mintry said she had to be in a wheelchair. The long walk and then standing and waving to all the people would have undone her.

She was so proud when Xander went forward carrying Hester. "All of you have met Princess Hester. Let me now show you each of the quadruplets. Their full names will be in all the news and vid data, along with their times of birth."

Everything went smoothly until the last few minutes when the High Priest anointed each of the four newborns. Everyone's attention was on them. Hester wiggled over to where the bowl of oil was. The next thing everyone witnessed was that she was wearing the bowl upside down on her head and she was halfway up the railing of the balcony. Her little silver wings sprouted out her back, and she flew over everyone's heads, then landed gently in her mommy's lap.

Initially, the loud gasp from the people below alerted them to her actions. Then a child's voice could be heard, "Mommy, she can fly."

Iona hugged Hessie and looked at Xander. Neither had been told she had sprouted wings.

King Xander went to the railing and raised his hands and palms out to the people, gesturing for them to quiet down so he could speak.

"Yes, Princess Hester can fly. We expect the others to do so as well. I and Queen Iona also can fly. Several of you can, but don't know how to activate your wings. There will be two schools opening soon. One is for children and the other for adults. These schools will be here in the capital. If they are successful, then others will be built in all the provinces. There will be some prep work that will have to be done, and that will be broadcast throughout Xandavier for all. If you have questions, please send them through com link 'attention flight.' The address will be sent out. Do not expect an answer immediately. But an answer will be forthcoming."

He waved to the people, then escorted everyone into the palace. To the noise of a huge party taking place outside the castle.

Two Years Later

All provinces had successful flight schools. The Xian's were coming into their own again. The skies were full of dragons. The Croffers and the Xian had made peace and were the allies they were meant to be. The royal family quietly sought out word on the Fire Emerald.

I n their late youth Princes Manier and Ranin began dreaming of a planet with a cave that glittered with jewels and diamonds with a giant emerald sitting on a pedestal.

A Sneak Peek

Fire Emerald

Chronicles of Xandavier Part 2

Twenty-five Years Later
The Prophecy of the Fire Emerald

That what had been lost those thousands of years ago will come back. When the Fire Emerald was restored to Xian, Xandavier will become the place of healing for all peoples.

It had been rumored that Queen Iona would find the Fire Emerald. But as time passed by, she was not the one to go. The world recognized her place was beside her King and children. She never strayed far from either.

Their children followed all the training from their Gods-Parents, absorbed the gifts they were each meant to receive. Recorded all the stories that were told about the Fire Emerald.

When they were ten, Manier and Ranin began to dream of the Fire Emerald. At first it was observing others near it, then it progressed to dream-walking around the cavern where it is worshiped on a distant planet.

The Fire Emerald was on a pedestal near the center of the cavern. The walls sparkled with diamonds, rubies, gold, and silver in the lights illuminating the precious stone. There were small wooden altars established in various natural alcoves; one was more ornate than the others. The only ones to came to this one was two young females, accompanied by five guards each. Even at the age of ten the brothers recognized them instantly—their life-mates.

The people worshiping were dressed in what they came to learn over yars were made of the most expensive fabric. Some worshipers gifted plates and bowls of food, others added people for the priests to use for their needs and pleasure.

In their dreams, when they walked among the people, they could hear the prayers, see their actions. The last two times they came near the emerald, they each heard a whisper, "Come for us. It is time."

"Us. Did you say 'us?'" Both brothers looked at one another, then at the emerald.

"Yes, I did. Princesses Syla and Anya are in grave danger. Only you can save them. If they are harmed, I will be destroyed. Come quickly."

In unison, the two answered, "We will come."

They woke instantly and went to their parents, explained what had happened. Their parents told them they had a visit from Goddess Oline and God Selenia. They had spoken about a quest the two young princes must go on.

Xander and Iona looked at one another. Xander spoke for them both. "Sons chose the warriors you want to accompany you and select the starship you will take. Ensure you take extra supplies. You don't know the distance you will travel.

"The God Selenia and Goddess Oline said the emerald will guide you. And that it is a treacherous quest that calls you. You are ready. The arduous training you have been through was to prepare for this specific journey. Do not let your guard down. Some you encounter will look crazed and ferocious, yet they are innocent, placed there to help; whereas others will look harmless and innocent. They mean to destroy you. Remember your training.

"You go with our blessings and prayers."

Two days later, Manier and Ranin returned to their parents. "We don't know what is going on. We have not dreamed of the fire emerald since we told it we would come."

Before either parent could answer, the God Selenia and Goddess Oline appeared. "It is saving its strength to guide you. The priests want to break it up and send pieces of it out to other places, believing that it would heal those in a particular area. But if they do the emerald will not be able to heal itself from the damage they do. So far, the High Priest has stopped them, but his time is near and when he leaves his world, the others will not be hindered.

Three Months Later

Kneeling before their parents, Manier and Ranin stood after they said a blessing over them. They turned and faced the people of their world. Manier stepped toward the mic, "We go to retrieve the Fire Emerald, and our life-mates. The prophecy will be fulfilled that Xandavier is a place a healing for all when we return."

Both transformed into dragons and flew off to their starship, Seeker II, as the crowds cheered.

About the author

Kathleen served in the Air Force for over twenty years. Her writing covers several genres: Romance, Science Fiction, Alien Romance Sci-Fi, Comedy, Paranormal, and realism. She and her husband of forty-eight years, have two children, five grandchildren, and three great-grandchildren. They live in the city of Show Low, in the White Mountains of northeastern Arizona with their three dogs; they call the girls—Sugar Pearl, Ruby Tuesday, and Gigi Lynn.

She is the founder of an organized group of writers, Transcendent Authors. Together they write and compile anthologies. They have produced and published six anthologies, with the seventh due out November 2024. The current ones available are *Tolerance: A Collection of Short Stories, Autumn—An Anthology,*

Spring: The Unexpected, Winter—An Ending and a Promise, Summer—When Doors Open, and *Deceit.* The next book is called *Fate—And all that Jazz.*

Her next novel, *Dream Brides, Part 1,* will released in the fall of 2024.

Kathleen's novel, *King of Onus, Book One of the Onus Chronicles* was published December 2023 and can be found on Amazon.com in Kindle, Kindle Unlimited, paperback, and hardcover.

She is the president of the White Mountains Chapter of Arizona Professional Writers. President of the Festival of Books.

You can reach her at www.kathleen-osborne.com or kathleen@kathleen-osborne.com.

Made in the USA
Middletown, DE
06 October 2024